THE LAST HERO

Innocent, convicted and condemned to die, Jesse Ringo showed no emotion as he set out on his walk to the gallows of Ellison jail. When the warden offered him a way out, he found himself riding alone on a mission only a fool — or a man with nothing to lose — would undertake. Ringo knew this was just a slower way to die, but with luck and a fast gun he would take plenty of Wyoming's real hellions with him.

DEMPSEY CLAY

THE LAST HERO

Complete and Unabridged

LINFORD
Leicester

First published in Great Britain in 2005 by
Robert Hale Limited
London

First Linford Edition
published 2006
by arrangement with
Robert Hale Limited
London

British Library CIP Data

Clay, Dempsey
    The last hero.—Large print ed.—
Linford western library
1. Western stories
2. Large type books
I. Title
823.9'2 [F]

ISBN 1–84617–241–1

Published by
F. A. Thorpe (Publishing)
Anstey, Leicestershire

Set by Words & Graphics Ltd.
Anstey, Leicestershire
Printed and bound in Great Britain by
T. J. International Ltd., Padstow, Cornwall

This book is printed on acid-free paper

1

KILLER'S REPRIEVE

They watched him go by their steel-barred doors, the losers, the rapists, the mad dogs and the truly lost. They wanted to offer some kind of encouragement as he went by, flanked by six of the pen's biggest bulls on his last walk, but they didn't. Jesse Ringo had not been in the Death House long before the warden decreed he should swing, but it was long enough for men with names like Skull Jones, Bloody-Handed Henry and Strangler to realize that the man who'd killed Brock Mitchell was not the kind who looked for sympathy or even wanted it. Ringo was different. He seemed fashioned out of something tougher than mere blood and bone, or at least this was the impression he'd conveyed to a sinister collection of bandits, thieves, garrotters, kidnappers and one demented bomb-blasting assassin, all waiting their appointment with scaffold, rope and masked executioner.

They respected this lean-bodied man with the rippling silent walk, but they did not know him. He had not let them. In the Death House of Ellison jail, Wyoming Territory, this doomed one had imposed his own solitary confinement. They dipped their hats to Ringo who thus far along his final journey was acting as though he didn't give one sweet damn that men were readying to sling a rough noose around his neck and drop him into eternity. Their hope was that he would maintain his air of flinty indifference right to the end. It gave these human vermin pride in their murderous profession to see one of their own play out the final act with such total aplomb. Made a man feel good to be a throat-slitting son of a bitch. Almost.

And each could only secretly pray to whatever dark god he worshipped that he in turn might find this same kind of strength when his time came. As that time surely would. There was but one way out of the Death House and that was in the grisly final embrace of Madam Hemp.

'There it is, bucko,' hissed the hulking head guard as the party rounded a corner to bring the scarred green door in sight. 'You wanna get the door?' Another guard sniggered. They were sadists in here, were paid to be. They saw so many go to their deaths, were so calloused and hardened by their occupation, that they wanted more than just snapping necks and gargling death rattles. They looked for men to crack, to break down and cry, fall on their goddamn knees and beseech Jesus, their mothers or the President of the United States to please have mercy and deliver them from all harm.

But they didn't really expect much from this man who walked so much like a wolf, and that was how it was. Ringo seemed locked in a private world of his own where nobody could make contact. And right now contact was the last thing he wanted.

This was an evil place where the lingering presence of death was almost tangible. Long after a hanging, the very air seemed poisoned by the horror and the terror of the newly dead. The stench of fear is said to be imaginary, but here it was all too real.

The green door creaked open and the party passed into the Gallows Room. Now a deep, sucked-out silence descended over the tiers as the caged ones listened for the muted clang of the opening trapdoor, which was the sound that would tell them that the death sentence passed upon Jesse Ringo by the 11th District Court of Wyoming Territory for the wilful murder of one Brock Mitchell late of Alameda had been carried out by the officials responsible for such matters in this place, namely Nathan Armstrong, warden of Ellison jail, and the institutional hangman.

No one knew the hangman's name.

Once, sometimes twice weekly, this lean, anonymous-looking man would drive up to the prison in his buggy with his black leather bag at his knees, to be admitted immediately and shown through to the Death House. Thorough, brisk and unfailingly efficient, he would spend several hours checking out his equipment and ensuring lever, trapdoor, rope and cross-beam were all in perfect working order before donning black smock and peaked hood.

This done, the warden would parade the executioner along every grim tier in the prison before personally escorting him back to the Gallows Chamber. This was a ritual performed deliberately to remind every inmate of the fate awaiting each and every one who had been tried and found guilty of the heinous crime of murder.

Just how heinous had been the sixgun slaying of wealthy import agent Mitchell by Ringo was still a matter of wide speculation throughout the Territory.

That Jesse Ringo had killed the big

5

man there was no doubt. But circumstances alter cases, and in the Mitchell — Ringo case these circumstances had appeared shady and unsavoury to say the least.

A young woman of Sioux blood had been brutally raped and murdered in Alameda, resulting in Brock Mitchell being arrested, charged and brought to trial for the crime. The press, prosecution and seemingly most of the Territory believed Mitchell guilty. Yet when a carefully selected redneck jury brought in a not guilty verdict before a blatantly racist judge, the big man walked free to boast publicly later that for him to have been strung up for ending the life of a 'red whore' would have been a disgrace and a travesty.

Two nights later, Jesse Ringo drifted into town on a yellow horse, forced Mitchell to draw his gun in self-defence and shot him down on the main street. Justifiable homicide! trumpeted the populist press, but the racist legal system decided it was murder. And so on this day the executioner was once again summoned to Ellison where he now stood waiting upon that high platform thirteen steps above the Gallows Chamber floor as Ringo halted to gaze upwards. Frozen eye met frozen eye as killer and executioner traded looks.

Nothing new for either man here today. Death was an old acquaintance for both, and its presence here in this tall, stone-walled chamber with weak sunlight filtering through high barred windows, though chilling to most present, appeared to affect the principal protagonists not at all.

'Ready?' asked the head guard of his expressionless charge.

'I was born ready, Jackson,' came the cool response. 'What are we waiting for?' This was breathtaking stuff, although half-expected by some present and particularly those who'd seen the condemned killer in the exercise yard stripped to the waist. Ringo's muscular torso was liberally scarred by blade, arrow, bullet, lash and flame yet surely even this graphic evidence of a violent life was insufficient to explain such laconic indifference to death by hanging?

Yet, as strong men gasped and the condemned flexed his supple shoulders, Warden Armstrong and his guest, a Mr Carmody from out of town, appeared paradoxically excited, almost as though they found something laudable in the killer's courage.

But how could this be? Even if Ringo might be widely viewed as a just avenger by most of the Territory today, the authorities deemed him guilty. In which case why should warden and impressive guest seem to be reacting to the condemned man's bravado in this puzzling manner?

Yet when Carmody suddenly spoke again his words seemed to convey a totally different impression.

'Thirteen steps if you're counting, killer,' he said with mocking relish. 'Think you'll make it?'

Ringo turned his head slowly.

The moment he focused on the warden's distinguished companion, memory kicked in. The white-painted courthouse in redneck Alameda. A hundred nobodies calling for his acquittal and a red-nosed judge and a hand-picked jury of good old boys finding otherwise. And amongst the waddies, Cousin Jacks miners, the wranglers, clerks, counter-jumpers, the victim's friends and the dead man's kin, one tall and impressive-looking man who hadn't seemed to fit.

It was this very same man who now smirked down at him from the observation platform in the dark heart of the stone house.

Mocking him. Sharing smiles with fat Armstrong. How come? Why was he even here? Carmody was the final jarring note on this the darkest and last of all his days.

Ringo felt anger rising but checked himself. He'd maintained his Indian-like stoicism and impassive calm through the last ten days of hell; he could stretch

9

it to cover the last few minutes.

He mounted the steep wooden steps smartly and without assistance, forcing his escorts to puff and pant as they hurried to maintain formation.

And now he stood upon the fatal trap, a young man in the prime of his manhood, his outward stoicism impressive but raging within himself and unable to deny the sensation of cold hands pressing down upon his diaphragm as though trying to force a desperate plea for mercy upwards and out of his throat.

So this was dying, he told himself as again he met the masked man's eyes. Seemed pretty overrated.

'Hood or otherwise?' The hangman was all brisk business.

He shook his head. 'Get on with it, loser. I don't have all day.'

Gasps of admiration were heard from below and the executioner breathed a curse. This one was making a mockery of the solemnity of both the occasion and his own status. Why wasn't Ringo breaking down in terror as even the hardest and the worst invariably did in these final desperate minutes? With angry jerky movements the hangman dropped the noose over Ringo's neck and was actually drawing it snugly and none too gently tight beneath a flinty jaw when the bombshell dropped.

'Thank you, hangman, that will be all for today,' the warden announced abruptly from below. 'Guards, kindly escort the prisoner to my office at once. There will be no execution of Prisoner Ringo today, possibly not at all in light of this stay of execution order from the Territorial Governor delivered into my hand one hour ago.'

So saying he held aloft an official-looking sheet of parchment boldly marked with the blood-red territorial seal for all to see, inmates and officials alike. In the stunned silence that followed, the warden's mysterious companion stared up fixedly at Ringo with a strange mixture of mockery and smug satisfaction working his features, suggesting that what was taking place here came as no surprise to 'Mr Carmody'.

'Well, don't just stand there,' Armstrong barked impatiently. 'Didn't you hear what I said?'

They had heard well enough but seemed to be having difficulty in comprehending. Then the authoritative sound of the warden slapping fat palms together jolted the dazed executioner into action. Fumblingly he removed his noose, and the prisoner was hauled back towards the steps. This surely was the most astonishing incident in the history of the Death House, and while Armstrong and his guest appeared paradoxically cheerful and buoyant about it, with hangman and guards predictably confounded, only the glitter of steel-blue eyes and the writhing of lean jaw muscles of one man betrayed total rage. That man was Jesse Ringo who had just been plucked from the jaws of death.

He knew this had to be some kind of cruel inhuman game being played upon him. There could be no other explanation.

★ ★ ★

They gave him a cigarette. The man named Carmody even lit it for him while the warden beamed fatuously across his big mahogany desk. Only two husky guards remained within the office, the others having been relegated to the outer room. Big mistake, Ringo was thinking as he drew deeply and took the good smoke deep into his chest. This made their second. Mistake number one had been their decision to play some filthy sadistic game with a man like himself. Life had made him as hard as a man could be, yet he was straight as a rifle barrel. He could never lead a man right to the very teetering brink of death only to pull him back at the last split second, and imply: 'Sorry, maybe later.' That was the sort of cruelty that would impress even a Cheyenne medicine man.

'I do believe he's in a state of shock, Carmody,' chuckled the warden, a large rotund man who sported mutton-chop whiskers and radiated an air of self-importance. He leaned forward to rest elbows on the blotter and his smile grew even wider.

'It's all right, Ringo. You can stop looking so damned suspicious. You really have survived — this isn't a dream.'

'Neither's this.'

Ringo came out of the chair in one fluent motion with his head tucked low to smash his crown into Armstrong's forehead, the impact belting the man clear out of his chair to go down backwards like a gunshot victim.

★   ★   ★

Ringo was attempting to get round the desk to bring his boots into play when the guards reached him, raging and snarling as they crashed big black billyclubs down on his head and shoulders. He was semi-conscious yet still swinging viciously when Carmody intervened.

'Cut it!' the man shouted at the guards. He gave the order with a natural authority that just had to be obeyed. 'Return him to his chair and fetch water for the warden.'

With blood streaming from his scalp and seeing double, Ringo still had to be restrained once they'd flung him back into his chair. Only when a length of rope was looped around his torso anchoring him to the chair did he stop struggling even though his look still said murder.

It was several minutes before order was restored and Warden Armstrong was able to sit up unaided. He fixed the prisoner with blurred eyes.

'He . . . he really is just a mad dog, Carmody,' he accused. 'Dammit, we've plainly made a vast mistake after all.'

'Take it easy, Warden,' said Carmody in his unflappable way. The man was all manners and style and yet, you sensed, underneath as hard as the very hobs of hell. 'Let's not leap to judgement. I'm quite sure Jesse can explain his seemingly base ingratitude at having been plucked from the very jaws of death. Isn't this so, killer?'

'Open a vein,' Ringo panted.

'Why,' persisted the tall man, 'did you attack the warden for doing you the greatest kindness anyone has done you in all your murky life?'

Ringo chose to answer straight.

'I know this game, it's called twist-the-knife. You've got a man at your mercy and ready to die, but you don't want to let him off the hook so easy. So instead of killing him clean you twist the knife in his guts. That's what hauling me off the scaffold was. So now I owe you both, and with luck I'll get to even scores with you next, you goddamn nancy!'

'What did I tell you, Warden?' Carmody said enthusiastically. 'We've made no error of judgement at all. Given the circumstances, the subject's violent reaction was something we should have anticipated.'

Armstrong looked dazedly unconvinced while Jesse Ringo was beginning to get the sure whiff of something very odd. Suddenly he was somebody called 'the subject' — like he was a specimen under a microscope. And the more he saw of this Carmody in action the more convinced he became that this was a big player from the main game — whatever that game might be. And hard. He never made a mistake in assessing a man.

As though reading his thoughts a suddenly sober Carmody turned back to him.

'An understandable reaction but totally wrong, Ringo. Between us, the warden and I are offering you the greatest chance any man was ever given. We are not merely offering you a reprieve from your justly deserved punishment, mister, we're offering you your freedom and your life, providing we can come to an understanding. Do you comprehend what I'm saying? This is miracle day for you. Your execution has been delayed by governmental edict and your full pardon can be secured providing you agree to undertake a simple job of work for, shall we say, Uncle Sam? So, now you have some idea what this is all about, what is your response?'

Ringo was silent for a long minute, studying the tall man. He sensed he could be sincere, even if totally ruthless. He wanted to tell him to go fry, maybe hand him a head-butt too if they'd only untie him. Yet undercutting his emotion, the magic word 'life' was working on him. The prospect of survival for a man plucked from the very noose itself was like an elixir of the gods.

But, weakening as he was, he was still cynical.

'So, who do I have to kill to win the cigar?'

Carmody straightened and glanced at the warden.

'How very perceptive, wouldn't you

agree, Armstrong?' Then without waiting for an answer, he added: 'All right, I think we understand one another, Jesse. There is something we would like you to do for us in return for our kindness — something which we believe only a man like yourself can handle. Shall I explain or would I be wasting my valuable time?'

Ringo nodded as slow understanding dawned. He was starting to believe this man, to sense there had been a great deal more more behind his 'rescue' than simple malice or a sadistic impulse to inflict an even greater punishment upon him than by holding the promise of life beneath his nose.

He was also beginning to sense it might well be his reputation as scout, troubleshooter and peacemaker — all of which had attracted wide publicity during his trial — that interested this man, although why he had yet to understand.

Carmody's next words suggested he might be getting close to the truth.

'I saw you quite by chance at your trial in Alameda,' the man revealed, resting against the desk while the warden dabbed at his ruined nose. 'Your so-called crime was plainly justifiable homicide, of course. Your misfortune was that you duelled with a man for killing an Indian and came up against an Indian-hating court, is all. What attracted me to the case initially was the immense publicity the press gave to your background as some kind of Daniel Boon of the Free Lands: scout, wagon master, hunter . . . even peacemaker, for Pete's sake. I must say the press really did seem to go overboard about someone whom I would regard with great suspicion as a man far too fond of settling matters with guns, and probably far too sympathetic to Indians and former slaves for polite society. Do you think I'd be justified in getting this impression?'

Ringo was slowly unwinding. He'd met this breed before. They were fed

arrogance and power with their mother's milk.

'I thought you wanted to talk,' he
grunted. 'So why don't you do it
instead of just blowing?'

The tall man half-smiled.

'Excellent, excellent.' He half-turned
to glance at the battered warden. 'You
can understand our interest in this one
now, surely, Warden? He's no fool. All
these attributes topped off by a name
for decency and honesty — despite a
murder charge, that is.'

'There was no murder,' Ringo growled.
'It was a duel in front of a hundred
eye-witnesses, like you know, desk cowboy.'

'See what I mean?' Carmody grinned
at a sullen Armstrong. 'Almost over
qualified for a certain kind of undertak-
ing, wouldn't you agree?'

Armstrong's response was a grunt
and a baleful stare at Ringo through
eyes already beginning to blacken.

Carmody turned back to Ringo.

'Enough small talk. You should know
that the organization I represent became

keenly interested in you during your trial, and the more our research turned up on Mr Jesse Ringo the more certain we became that you could be the one man best suited by temperament, experience and background to be of a great assistance to us.'

He spread his hands wide.

'We could have extricated you from your situation and exposed your trial for the farce it was much earlier than this, I must now confess. But I had to be sure. It was necessary for me to see you exposed to the ultimate terror before I could be sure that you were as ideal as you appeared. I'm happy to say you came through with flying colors.'

A silence fell.

Then Ringo said: 'Some test.' His eyes narrowed. 'Tell me, what would have happened if I'd failed?'

'You'd be dead. As it is, you stand on the threshold of an opportunity which, should you complete it as envisioned, will not only earn you substantial cash money but a full governor's pardon for the killing of that rapist you smoked at Alameda. So tell me, killer, am I capturing your interest or not?'

By this Ringo could actually sense the shadow of the gallows receding further away from him. Everything was beginning to tally at last, make some kind of sense. This man wanted him so badly he had secured a pardon for him and had even involved the warden of a penitentiary in this final brutal test on the gibbet. He caught the whiff of real power, something infinitely bigger than anything he'd ever encountered before. And something else, very much something else about Mr Carmody.

His features remained unreadable.

'Explain.'

Carmody obliged. Ringo would be required to travel to an as yet unidentified destination where his assignment, which he revealed broadly would take him back to the sprawling Free Lands of his youth, would involve investigations, action and certainly a high degree of danger.

When he asked who he would be working for, Carmody seemed surprisingly frank. His employer would be the Chief of Security at a secret and anonymous branch of the Department of War located in Sweetgrass.

He was impressed despite himself when Carmody produced official documentation and a heavy steel badge to support his claim of working for Uncle Sam. Then the man really showed his authority by ordering his manacles removed, after which he escorted him alone from the warden's office to the gatehouse where an unguarded door stood open to the big free world outside.

As they strolled out into the open Carmody fingered a cigar from an inner pocket and set it alight.

'Everything I've told you is genuine, mister,' he said. 'You must know that your once peaceful Free Lands have been racked by gunrunning, rustling, gang war and bloody murder over the past year. They claim you know that country better than any white man living, so we'll be giving you a chance to prove it. But before we shake hands it's essential you realize that the skill which interests the government most of all at this time is your guts and ability to survive. I trust you fully understand this?'

'Mebbe.'

'You see, we perceive that the criminals and outlaws who've been defying us and creating such havoc are now in danger of setting the entire frontier ablaze, and more than ever we are driven to fight fire with fire. Your work is bound to be dangerous. But of course you are still free to decline.'

Ringo almost smiled. Sure. Decline and most likely keep a second appointment with the hangman. He nodded and the man who'd saved his life smiled. A tall smooth man whose face you couldn't read, polished, educated and plausible, and yet, Ringo sensed, underneath as cold and ruthless as any kill-crazy two-gunner he'd ever known.

But not even that would stop him from grabbing at his big chance with both hands.

★   ★   ★

Ringo never knew if what he encountered when they reached the anonymous-looking building called the Agency in Greenfield, was accidental or otherwise: Agency — an innocuous name for an undercover government bureau involved in security — was apparently the sort of place where the right hand was rarely privy to what the left might be doing at any given time.

The journey south from the pen had been uneventful except perhaps for some dark and unwelcome thoughts that rose unbidden to tease at the edges of Ringo's resolve.

They were brutal, basic and elemental. Namely, kill Carmody and simply disappear. He could have done it easily. Carmody wouldn't stand a prayer against him despite the fact that he was unarmed and the other was not. It was tempting, but only up to a point.

For one thing, he'd never killed in cold blood.

Even more important, he had no desire to spend the rest of his life running from a rope, as would be inevitable if he took this man out.

As he willed his way out of the brief temptation, he admitted to himself that he was genuinely intrigued by the prospect of working in the troubled Free Lands again, this time for Uncle Sam. He liked the sound of the word 'security'. Then, of course, there was the sweetener. Carmody, speaking for Agency, was assuring him a governor's full pardon and clean slate as part reward for his one job of work. Better to find out whether the task was achievable before doing something that could have every badge, bounty hunter, town sheriff, trooper, vigilante and government dick in the territory hunting Jesse Ringo.

When first confronted by the quiet-looking building set on a shady back street of Greengrass flanked by a horse corral on one side and a dry-goods store on the other, he reckoned everything looked pretty ordinary and unremarkable.

That impression changed as the two men made their way through the first two heavily guarded doors to a large, sprawling building with thick walls and small windows. More flinty-looking men with guns could be glimpsed along the green-painted corridor with rooms leading off on both sides.

Apparently nobody had forewarned the strongman whom Carmody called Herman that Ringo was the proddy type.

Herman was duty officer at Agency and took his job very seriously. The close-cropped heavyweight greeted Carmody respectfully but plainly didn't take to the cut of Ringo's jib.

'Just a minute while I check you out, pal,' he growled, blocking access to the passageway with his heavy bulk. He immediately began running hands as big and hairy as beavers over Ringo, was none too gentle about it either.

'I'm not toting,' Ringo said.

'I'll be the judge of that,' said Herman, gusting unpleasant breath into his face. 'Give me your boots.'

'What?'

'You deaf or somethin'? Your boots, feller. You'd be amazed what shifty bastards try and sneak in here in their footwear. C'mon, c'mon, I don't have all day.' Ringo looked a question at Carmody who appeared detached and faintly amused. He stared big Herman straight in the eyes.

'Your fat ass,' he said softly. Herman's rage was immediate, the huge hands incredibly swift.

Ringo swayed smoothly back out of reach in one supple motion. Herman lunged for him, red-faced and snarling. Ringo assessed the bulge of big thigh muscles as they bunched and thrust all that meaty bulk forward, read the

29

forward motion accurately, kept a wary eye on those outsized hands.

This assessment was made in a fraction of a second. In the fraction that followed, Ringo allowed the man to come to him. At the moment of contact his right boot lifted and pistoned squarely into Herman's gut with sickening force. The breath gushed out of the man and he yelled in shock as hands, astonishingly strong, lifted him off the floor in a wrestler's grip, then flipped his great mass over one shoulder with ridiculous ease to ram him headlong into the heavy metal doors which had been locked behind them after they came through.

The entire building shook to the impact and Herman the heavyweight crashed on to his back and lay twitching and hissing like a beached whale.

Ringo deliberately stood on an extended hand and put all his weight upon it. Even unconscious, Herman screamed like a woman until a kick in the teeth chopped off the sound.

'What the devil is going on out here?'

The man who burst from a side door flanked by hard-faced men with guns had authority stamped all over him. Instinct warned Ringo that this had to be the boss whom Carmody had told him about. Westerman. The Chief. Head of Agency, the confidante of governors and senators and no stranger in the halls of power in Washington, or so it was claimed.

And Jesse Ringo's new employer?

Maybe.

By the time Carmody had soothed his superior's ruffled feathers and the bodyguards had dispersed, their places in the inner sanctum taken by bustling aides who spread maps all about the big roomy office, some calm had returned. After the dust had settled the new recruit was formally welcomed by a sober Westerman, who immediately got right down to business.

He started off by confirming officially that Ringo — should he prove acceptable — was slotted for the assignment in the sprawling Free Lands, which encompassed both the Crystal Basin and Creation Mountain regions of the Territory with which he was known to be familiar.

Westerman continued to furnish details while Ringo sat puffing on one of his coronas. An attentive Carmody indicated salient dots on the maps with a leather-covered stick as the briefing continued.

As Carmody had hinted earlier the troubles had all started with guns. Weapons had come pouring into the Free Lands from unknown sources and it was suspected that the supplier was trading with several warring tribes, Cheyenne, Sioux and Crow as well as the numerous outlaw bands that had begun polluting the once pristine and peaceful dangerous sector of the territory.

'For some considerable time we were focusing on a shadowy operator by the name of Helmut Haines, who adopted several effective aliases in his career,' the Chief supplied, studying Ringo closely now. 'Haines was our strongest suspect and we were hunting him vigorously but with little success until several months ago when someone in his organization informed on him. We staged an ambush in which Haines perished. We hoped this would put an end to the gun-running but the opposite proved to be the case. His successors, whoever they may be, have proved far more active and elusive even than he. But gun-running, so we were soon to become aware, merely seemed to open the floodgates to wider problems as authority in the region diminished. Rustling is on the increase now and because of the breakdown of law enforcement in the region Agency was forced to increase its men in the field. Subsequently we lost several hand-picked men in our operations and the situation is worsening every day.'

Carmody folded his arms and half smiled.

'I'm sure you now fully understand

why we were prepared to go to such lengths to recruit a man of your unique qualifications, Ringo.'

'So,' drawled Ringo, studying his cigar, 'who do you want me to kill first?'

'This seems to be a catch phrase of his, Chief,' supplied an acerbic Carmody. 'I think his intention is to shock.'

'Dogs bark and killers talk tough,' the head man said dismissively. 'In answer to your question, Mr Ringo, whom you kill — or even whether indeed you kill anyone — will depend on events and progress when you follow up all the additional information with which Intelligence will supply you. Suffice to say that at this early stage we believe Haines operated a large and highly effective operation and was possibly survived by others including his wife, who just might know something about his illegal networks of crime. That is for you to find out. To summarize your briefing, we want to stop the flow of rifles and we don't give a rap who or how many you might have to kill to achieve these ends.'

It was a fine cigar.

Ringo liked wild women, strong whiskey, good cigars and guns. He was prepared to accept the assignment, he advised. He'd had wide experience with rustlers but was obliged to point out he knew little about arms smuggling and therefore would require some briefing.

Westermen nodded approvingly. He thought the man from Ellison jail sounded professional.

'We've anticipated you, sir,' he said firmly, folding his arms and biting into a freshly lighted stogie. 'We've arranged for you to visit Fort Despair where you'll find a gentleman named Osage Smith waiting for you. Name ring a bell?'

Ringo nodded. Osage, an aging fellow-scout who knew the Free Lands inside and out, would be a valuable ally.

'I've done manhunting before,' he stated. 'But not for the government. When and if I catch up with these outlaws — '

'You won't be squeamish,' Carmody stated flatly.

'We're overworked and under-staffed,' Westerman stated, his stare boring hard. 'And arrested men can slip the law, you're living proof of that.' A pause. 'Dead men never do. Do you understand what we are saying, mister?'

Ringo felt a chill. It was clear enough. This outfit played the game hard. He shrugged the thought away.

'Smith makes a difference,' he remarked. He paused. 'Anything else I should know about this job?'

'Just that we don't accept failure,' Carmody said coldly. A deliberate pause. 'Nor do we tolerate it.'

The implied threat was plain. The irony was that it was unnecessary. His promised reward guaranteed his total commitment. He didn't intend welshing on the deal then spending the rest of his life running from the law. He had no option but to play by their rules, lethal though they might be. He rose and reached for his hat.

'OK, I'm in.'

It took less than half an hour to swear

him in and issue his equipment. Only then did Westerman manage a smile.

'So . . . welcome aboard — killer.'

'Takes one to know one I always say.'

They didn't like that. But he wasn't doing this to make friends. He was working to redeem his own life.

2

TIGER BY THE TAIL

Such a pretty day to be riding north upon such risky business!

But Jesse Ringo was accustomed to such ironies in his life and found it easy to relax in the saddle and drink in the familiar high plains landscapes with little thought for what might lie ahead of him at Fort Despair. He absorbed the breathtaking vistas with the passion and intensity that only a man who'd actually slipped from under the very shadow of death might, as he let the winding trail carry him down out of rolling hills towards the water.

To the west now lay the blue lakes, shimmering like the ocean, to the east wooded escarpments clothed in the colours of late fall. A north-easterly was blowing in the mid-afternoon and little waves lapped peacefully against the rocks and flattened on narrow beaches of white sand.

The government horse he rode was ugly but sound; it moved easily beneath him as he held it to a steady lope. Familiar landmarks drew near, came abreast, fell away behind, all evoking memories.

The wanderer of the West was back in the land of his unique childhood, a deal of which had been spent along the far shores of these lakes where he had run Injun-wild and Injun-naked through the brush and tall grasses with other wild white and red boys his own age, unchecked and unsupervised by his offbeat artist parents who'd journeyed west from Brooklyn to paint the 'pristine wilderness', not to become tied down with child-rearing.

Eventually he came upon Indian fishermen netting from their canoes. They were peaceful Sioux, formerly of the reservations and long adjusted to government handouts with their glory days fading far behind.

He reined in to watch them dragging their nets closer to the shore, alive with shimmering silver. There was shouting and urgency amongst the fishermen, desperation for the fish which threshed and glittered under the westering sun, fighting for their lives in a way he could relate to this fine day.

The Sioux sighted him and waved. He did not return their greetings, but heeled the horse and left them behind. He was a white man who looked white, dressed white and sometimes acted white but underneath often thought and fought more like an Indian.

Along with the Indians' talent for hunting and fighting he'd learned from them the art of survival, as a matter of some necessity. Many a time he'd had to rely upon his own resources when his folks might suddenly disappear and leave him alone and largely unprovided for while they headed for the far horizons to paint a cuddly beaver family at play or maybe a good hanging.

A half-smile worked his mouth.

He loved Jacinta and Errol — wherever the hell they might be right now. But he was their opposite in just about every way that counted. In direct contrast to their careless bohemian lifestyle he'd grown up practical, hard-edged and more capable of looking out for himself than anybody twice his age had a right to be. There was no weakness in this man. He was as the land had shaped him, self-sufficient and independent, sure of himself and his abilities to survive.

'Come on, Gov,' he urged as he cleared the lakes' region to enter another line of hills. 'Sun's well down and we're not stopping tonight until we've got clean sheets and grain feed, so keep lifting them up and putting them down.'

Jesse Ringo raised the distant lights of Fort Despair at midnight and slept in a hotel room as he'd promised himself, drifting off with a huge Wyoming moon pouring metallic light through his

41

window, acutely aware that today was his first full day without pain, shackles, uncertainty or fear since the long nightmare had begun.

And so he slept peacefully in Fort Despair where law and order had become just empty words. Beyond, to the north, lay the beautiful and bloody Crystal Basin where outlaw wars nobody really understood were raging again, evil men were smuggling guns and thieving cattle and were growing rich and sometimes being murdered as they slept.

★ ★ ★

Carmody and Westerman silently studied their newest recruit. Agency fatalities were on the rise amongst those who worked in the field and the recruiting process for personnel was an ongoing burden in Sweetgrass.

Tucker was an infamous knifer from Nevada who appeared dull and brutish, yet his record proclaimed him to be clever, treacherous, evil-natured and an excellent sneak-killer. He in no way resembled the bravo breed of steely gunslinger like the last man hired, but was rather the kind of brute you sent in to discharge a contract with stealth, cunning and not a hint of squeamishness.

'I don't know . . . ' the Chief demurred. They were studying Tucker unobserved from a high window and could not be overheard. 'Bottom of the barrel stuff, wouldn't you agree?'

'We just lost two agents in that foul-up on the Pueblo Road,' Carmody reminded in his clipped, impersonal way. 'At the moment we can hardly afford to be choosy.'

Westerman perched on a desk top, hawkish, intelligent features framed by silver hair of senatorial length. The Agency boss was thoughtful as he folded his arms, tucking in white hands which had never committed a single violent action while he commanded one of the government's most ruthless bureaux.

'Perhaps I'm slipping into the error of comparing this one unfavourably with Monday's man.'

'Well, I'll concede that a Ringo this one ain't.'

'Ringo is a man.'

'Sure. But don't get carried away, Chief. We agreed we're not certain of that noose-cheater. But one look at this Neanderthal and you just know you can rely upon him to do anything, the uglier the better. Dependability, that's what I see when I look at this slaughterman.'

'I've seen the day when we'd sic the dogs on to something like this.'

Carmody's face turned cold.

'And I've seen the day when we couldn't get invited to a Cheyenne intelligence gathering. Now we're on first-name terms with legislators and railroad tycoons.'

The point was made. Westerman knew his lieutenant was right.

Carmody moved to the window and opened it. The man leaning against the wall in the room beneath blinked up at him from frog eyes fringed with greasy lank hair, thumbs hooked into a six-inch belt from which dangled no fewer than four wicked-looking knives, one the size of a Roman legionnaire's famed short sword.

'Tucker,' he ordered sharply. 'Kill that hatrack.'

The frog-eyed man palmed a throwing knife with silken speed, pivoted in shabby boots and his right arm blurred. There was a thud and the wooden hatrack clattered and tilted back into the corner with the blade buried two inches deep into the upright.

Carmody turned with elevated brows and Westerman made an impatient gesture.

'All right, all right, you've made your point. Send him to Training.' Carmody jerked a thumb and Tucker disappeared.

'Funny thing, Chief,' he commented, 'neither you nor I even considered recommending Ringo to Training, did we?'

'What can you train a tiger to do? Eat people? He already knows how.'

Carmody essayed a small smile as he went to the liquor cabinet and took down bottle and glasses. Hiring, firing and with ever-increasing frequency eliminating enemies of the government, was as much a part of everyday life for the Agency bosses as taking lunch. Routinely they dealt with enemies and informers, with men who could kill and men who had to die. The two shared a rare kind of cold-blooded detachment that identified them as even worse than the people they hired to handle their dirty work.

The attitude of Carmody and Westerman was that the Wyoming Territory was in danger of being torn apart by outlawry, which justified any act of retaliation and suppression on their part. Both had learned their basic trade in Army Intelligence during the Civil War but this was a more ruthless war and they were sworn to win it. They sipped their drinks like members of a plush leather-and-mahogany Cheyenne club.

But appearances could deceive.

At this time Agency was hanging by a thread. The outbreak of outlawry had become its responsibility, and Washington had recently made its position only too plain. Agency would either succeed or it would be wound up.

Carmody and Westerman would never let this happen.

During their tenure here they had enjoyed major successes which had resulted in ongoing promotions and salary hikes that found them now two of the highest paid active service officials in the country.

But the cost of maintaining their record in the face of the Free Lands situation had grown higher by the day. Brutal solutions they'd not have considered five years ago were now everyday occurrences and were now part of policy. And Agency basic policy could be summed up in a few words. Understand the problem, uncover the perpetrators, eliminate. What could be simpler?

No costly and cumbersome court trials, investigations, escapes, jailbreaks or innocence verdicts when a rustler or gunrunner was six feet under.

It was this brutally effective attitude that had seen Agency go to great pains to select a suitable 'tiger' for this all-important assignment, and they fully expected him to hunt and kill as ordered.

'I guess your tiger analogy does apply rather well to Jesse Ringo, Chief. I couldn't feel more confident. You too?'

'I would be reassured but for his eyes,' Westerman mused.'

'What about them?'

'He sees out but you can't see what's behind them. Like one-way glass. I've encountered a few like that, Carmody. You can never be totally certain just which way they will jump.'

Carmody was unperturbed.

'I see no complexity in Ringo, Chief. He's a man born to combat and violence. Research tells us that due to a lax upbringing and exposure to savages who schooled him in their ways, he was fighting and killing like a man while still a boy. His shortcomings appear to be a high sense of morality and at times he appears to see himself as some kind of warrior in the cause of justice. Rubbish, of course. But he's no fool.' He paused with a self-satisfied smirk. 'As effective and as uncomplicated as a scalping knife, that's how I see our tiger.'

'Then why do I still have this uneasy feeling we may be holding a tiger by the tail?'

*   *   *

Next evening was chill and blustery in the turpentine town sprawling at the foot of the denuded hill upon which stood the Blackfeet-torched ruins of the early fort which gave Fort Despair its name.

Trapping, hunting, mining and the wagon trade had created Fort Despair but in these uncertain times only the turpentine plant along the river was holding it together. The semi-respectable side of the town, that was. There would always be mountain men coming down to blow their season's earnings and there were enough saloons and dives to sustain a large floating population of gamblers, cons, drifters, saloon girls, gunmen and much worse.

Axemen and sawmen travelled further from town every year to fell the pines from which the turpentine was extracted at the plant before being shipped south by freighter. The cut-over land, the greying mountains of sawdust and the belching chimneys of the tin-roofed plant had succeeded in converting a once pretty settlement into a place that looked just about as rough and lawless as it really was. It was no place for the faint-hearted but was just about perfect for the hard-bitten three or four hundred who called it home.

Ringo's shirt was sticking to him as

he waited in the airless Blue Angel for the arrival of Osage Smith.

Agency had set up the reunion of the former fellow-scouts. They'd informed Ringo that although Smith had fallen on hard times he still retained their confidence. He understood Agency had recently attempted to tap into Smith for information concerning the gun-running, but refused to pay the extortionate fees he demanded. But when they came up with Ringo's name the man had agreed to parley.

Smith showed just as the sultry waitress with the cleavage brought Ringo's second glass of chilled local beer.

The beer was a pleasant surprise but Osage Smith proved a big disappointment. Glad enough to see him, maybe. But if Ringo had to find one word to describe his former rugged fellow-scout of the 6th Regiment, it was jittery.

Osage looked and sounded like a man living on the edge. He acted shifty and suspicious in comparison with his

51

younger, extroverted self. Yet plainly the man was doing all right in his natty grey suit and derby hat in a town where it was mainly moleskins, chinos, blue denim or calico.

'Hard times, Ringo boy,' he explained over their beer, eyes playing restlessly about the noisy barroom. 'Jumpy times up here these days for all sorts of operators, what with the gunrunning and rustler troubles and suchlike . . .' He paused to study Ringo with deep-set eyes.

'Hey, but it sure was one hell of a surprise to get word about you. I'd given you up for dead. Last I heard on you they'd nailed you for drilling some geezer and were slotted for the high walk. What happened?'

'A long story that would likely bore you to tears, Os. Anyway, I'm here now and looking for action. And whatever's brewing, I know you've got your finger on it as always. Right?'

'Could be, old son . . . just could be . . .'

Smith studied him with eyes that missed nothing. In their days with the regiment Osage was the hawkeye of the outfit, the shrewd head and the analyzer. Ringo, by contrast, was the one who took charge whenever danger threatened and the lives of a couple of scouting long riders were plainly on the line.

'So, just tell me exactly what brings you up here after all this time, Jesse? Apart from lookin' up old pards, that is.'

Ringo looked the man in the eye.

'Helmut Haines,' he said.

Osage Smith flinched and drew back a little. He glanced about sharply, squinting through the smoke-thickened air to see if anyone had overheard. Then he leaned closer and spoke in a low voice.

'Man, you don't just bust right out with a name like that in a place like this!'

'Why not?'

'Jeeze, you haven't changed any, have

you? Still go in as hard as ever ... '
Smith paused to light up a cigarette before continuing: 'What's your interest in this *hombre*?'

'He's dead.'

'So?'

'Who killed him?'

Ringo was not subtle and saw no reason to be. They were old pards. But it was a long time since they'd last cracked a cold one together, maybe too long. He could sense Osage Smith withdrawing from him without moving, saw his worn, pinched face closing over.

'It's been a long time, Ringo. Things change, people change.'

'You know about this gunrunner, I can tell. What is it about him that scares you? Like we know, the man is dead. How dangerous can a dead man be?'

Now Smith was physically distancing himself as he rose and stepped back. 'I need to check with some contacts, Ringo. Guys I know hereabouts who had connections with Haines. Can you give me, say, an hour?'

Ringo didn't want to give him five minutes. He'd have readily granted the old Os all the time he wanted but this was a different man. He was also the only contact he had in the region, and he had a real strong hunch he knew something vital.

'Don't let me down, Os. And there's dollars in this for you, remember?'

'Just you take it easy here,' Smith smiled. 'Best place in Fort to do it. They've got a dancer here who'll turn the brains of even a hard nut like you into mush. She'll be on soon, and she'll bring the roof down. By the time she's through and you've had a couple more I'll be back with something on your party you can hang your hat on. Stay easy.'

'You too . . . pard.'

Smith was gone and Ringo's glass was empty. He ordered another and leaned back. The longer he studied the faces of his fellow drinkers the more he realized all present appeared to be looking and acting exactly how you'd expect of folks in a dump like this place. It was Smith, his old trail pard, who was acting oddly, almost like a stranger.

Suddenly guitars thrummed loudly and a buzz of anticipation ran through the crowded room as a space was cleared by the bar into which abruptly appeared a barefooted girl in a skimpy costume of spangles and sequins that made it appear as if her voluptuous young body was on fire as she launched into her routine. The paying customers were roaring and stomping already. With other things occupying his mind it took Ringo longer to relax but eventually he realized he was enjoying himself.

She was not very talented, he could see, even though the mob was acting as though she were a prima ballerina having a top night on her slippered toes. Not so talented — but damned easy to watch, he decided. She was young and supple and made a man hungry. She rattled little castanets in her fingers as she rippled around the floor. She halted before Ringo's table and her hips swayed before him in easy, fluid movements. While her dark eyes held his, she ran her hands over her glistening body in a way that stirred him and stopped him wondering how Smith was making out.

For some reason, right at that moment, the full horror of what had befallen him in the gaunt grey tomb of Ellison jail hit him hard and seemed to add an edge to his appetites.

He winked and patted the empty chair beside him. She flashed her teeth at him before whirling away to finish her act with a series of whirling pirouettes that had the customers seeing her off in a virtual typhoon of applause.

Were they acknowledging her artistry or raw sex appeal, he wondered as he took out tobacco and papers.

He was licking his cigarette into a cylinder when a shadow fell across his table. He looked up and there she was, dressed for the street now in something dark and enveloping.

'You liked my dancing?' she smiled.

'More than liked.' He touched the back of the empty chair. 'Drink?'

Her name was Fay and she drank her liquor straight. She also talked straight, at least for a time. Then, as he was about to suggest they take a bottle or two to her place or his, she suddenly leaned close and squeezed his hand.

'Mr Smith wants you to follow me when I leave,' she whispered. 'He said to tell you he has the information you want, but it's too dangerous for him to return and be seen with you in public.'

She was up and gone in the blinking of an eye leaving him staring after her through smoke so thick you could cut chunks out of it and use it for curing ham. Directly behind his belt buckle the big ganglion of abdominal nerves was beginning to twitch and act up the way it often did when he found himself sampling air that carried the faint whiff of danger.

It was only intuition, he knew. Sometimes intuition was reliable, other times not worth a plugged nickel.

His gaze played over the sea of faces. It was OK. Everyone still appeared normal and relaxed. He was the only edgy one in the place.

He set his hat on his head and took his instincts for a walk.

* * *

When Ringo strode quickly to an alley-mouth shrouded in shadows he glimpsed two silhouettes receding along its dark length ahead of him, making for the next street.

It was dark, he'd just come out of the lighted saloon and his vision had not adjusted as yet. Even so he was still able to make out that one figure was female, possibly the dancer. Her male companion was roughly the same size and shape as Osage Smith.

What the hell was going on here?

'Hey!' he shouted, but they just kept running.

The girl was several paces ahead of

the man as they neared the far end of the alley at the run, but the man stubbed his toe on something in the dark, stumbled and almost fell. A curse drifted back. Not only looked like Smith but sounded like him also.

Strange and even stranger!

While experience was warning him that this situation smelt like week-old fish, Ringo was listening to different messages coming from his thinkbox. Osage was a pard. If he was running from something he must be scared, which meant he could use some help. Besides, that Fay had legs to die for.

He took off, palming his sixshooter as he lengthened his stride. He was half-way along the alley when both figures suddenly disappeared. He lifted his pace but kept closer to the wall. A sluggish cat barely escaped being tramped underfoot as he neared the corner. Halting, he thrust his head around and the thunder of a gunshot punched a fist-sized chunk of masonry out of the wall inches above his head.

Ringo dropped belly flat and triggered at the gunflash across the street where empty beer barrels stood piled up against the wall of a derelict saloon.

'Os!' he shouted. 'Is that you?'

The only response was the stutter of running feet coming from the direction of the narrow roadway beyond the darkened saloon. He triggered twice into the sky, the big head-jolting reports attracting another shot from the barrel stand, the bullet whining over his head.

Staves splintered and breaking old barrels crashed down under the volley he sent crashing back.

No response this time.

Refilling his weapon from his shell belt he broke from cover in a low crouch to leg it across the street, weaving and ducking, barely conscious of the startled citizens now following this deadly play from either size of the battle zone.

'Os!' he roared again. 'Answer me!'

Whoever answered did so with a rifle. Ringo swerved and dived headlong for the barrel pile. As he came up on one knee he heard receding running footsteps above the rasp of his own breathing. The stink of turpentine hit him thick and strong, but he didn't think much of it, this being a turpentine town.

When he caught his breath he darted off warily to enter this second, even gloomier alley with sixgun on full cock and cat-quick eyes darting every which way. The stink grew stronger and now he was slipping on something wet. He scooped up a bullet-splintered stave and flung it well ahead, but drew no further fire.

'Ringo! The bastards have got me!'

Smith's disembodied voice came to him from somewhere down the alley where the shadows lay thickest. Ringo went on in a low crouch, breathing hard, teeth locked. He slowed then stopped upon realizing the wetness on the ground was turpentine, and he was now splashing in it.

Alarm bells went off in his head a

moment before he glimpsed the dim but identifiable silhouette of a woman in a window hurling something that flickered and sputtered.

Ringo was spinning away when the blazing bottle of turpentine hit at his feet and broke, exploding the entire alleyway into a sea of raging flame.

Although instantly surrounded by fire, Ringo had been in full motion from the very moment the turpentine-soaked earth caught ablaze. With explosive agility he threw himself violently backward towards the old saloon in a series of giant flips which eventually saw him dive clear of the reaching flames with nothing worse than smoking pants and one burning boot, knowing it was far from over yet. He knew he'd been suckered in and and doubted the enemy was likely to rely solely upon the fire to finish him off.

Despite choking smoke, streaming eyes and boots as hot as the hobs of hell, he zigged and zagged frantically and so evaded the storm blast of sixgun and rifle fire which reached for him both from alley and street.

A last tremendous leap carried him over the pile of broken barrels. He hit the street with smoking pants legs and his hat gone somewhere. He somersaulted twice and came up in a crouch facing a startled man with a rifle who plainly had not expected him to survive the inferno and come hurtling over the barrels to appear less than thirty feet distant with a .45 in his fist and teeth snarling whitely in a blackened face.

They triggered together

A bullet grazed Ringo's shoulder. He staggered but didn't stop shooting. His first shot caught the rifleman low down somewhere, causing him to stumble. His next blew the crown of his head away and he flopped to the ground, convulsing and choking.

Ringo twisted away, beating at burning pants as he plunged back for the cover of the barrels again. The alleyway was an inferno by this time. That Fay had damn near done for him.

He knew it was her. Couldn't be two silhouettes like that in one dirty town.

People were yelling and screaming but he barely heard. He focused on the alley surrounds and immediately glimpsed a menacing silhouette perched up on a railing out of reach of the flames, head twisting from side to side, looking for him.

He lined up and touched off a single shot.

The report was followed by the dim thud of a falling body followed immediately by a blood curdling shriek as the wounded man tried to drag himself out of the fire.

He didn't make it.

Ringo scorched across open ground and cut past two buildings to throw a tight left into a laneway leading down to the building where he'd glimpsed Fay of the gorgeous legs and the talented throwing arm.

Two figures appeared scuttling for a darkened storehouse, one in a fluttering skirt.

'Freeze up!' he roared.

They ignored him. He fired two shots deliberately high to stop them. But a gap in a fence saw the woman dive through and vanish as the second figure picked up speed.

Ringo was cool as he dumped empty shells and reloaded and, on the run, he heard somewhere a door creak on rusted hinges. His attitude at such times was simplicity itself: You hurt me, sunshine, and I'll hurt you.

He supposed he was glad the double-crossing Fay had slipped away. He streaked by the fence gap to leap up on to the plankwalk, where he lunged for the gaping door.

He was not certain who'd ducked inside but if his instincts were sound the party would be wearing a derby hat and spats.

He barrelled through the entrance and hurled himself violently to one side so as to offer no silhouette. He was surprised to see dim lights and shabby, moving figures here and there. Looked like some kind of interior hobo jungle. They were moving about in the brown-tinted haze like spooks startled at a haunting.

'You bums, freeze and you might get to stay alive!' he roared. 'Move and you die!'

They might well be out of their skulls on sterno and wood alcohol but they recognized sudden death when it came busting in on them. So they froze. All but one.

A second door was opening slowly in a far corner. Ringo triggered first and spoke after.

'Os? That you?'

A sixgun flared in retaliation from the corner, and hoboes quaked in their broken-soled boots as the ricochet came off something metallic and zipped and zinged about the gloomy spaces like a demented insect.

The door was tugged again, more feebly this time. Keeping the point of his aim low, Ringo calmly punched off three evenly spaced shots, like a man test-firing a pistol to check the timing.

The thud of a falling body was followed by the convulsive stuttering of a boot-toe against tin.

'Stay froze, cousins,' he ordered, threading his light-footed way between their miserable little fires.

He grabbed up a grease-lamp and placed it upon a packing crate where it spilled greasy light over the spread-eagled figure and glistening white face of the man he had once ridden the river with, pards together.

Osage Smith's natty grey suit was soaked in dark blood, the jaunty derby nowhere to be seen. Doubtless the man was in great pain, and yet his overriding emotion appeared to be astonishment. Os appeared to be trying to figure out how it could be, that having gone to such desperate lengths to rid himself of his former saddle pardner he now found himself lying here with his life's blood soaking into a dirt floor and a 'stranger' standing over him with twin Colts angling down.

Ringo was indeed a stranger now. He would kill any man who tried to kill him. A friend who tried to kill him, he would kill twice.

'What the hell is this, Os? Might as well tell me as take it with you where it won't do either of us any good.'

'I'm s-sorry, Rin — '

'Don't give me that.' Ringo signalled a warning to the fleabag onlookers to relax, dropped to one knee. In the feeble light his face was like a gleaming knife blade. 'You've got to be working with the other side, that's the only thing that makes sense, man. I'm hunting gunrunners and rustlers, so you must be with them. Who are they?'

'You gotta believe I'm sorry, Jesse. You and me was true pards. But a man gets old and times get tough and — '

'I came to you like a pard and when you found out what I was after you whistled up your pals and the girl and set out to kill me. With guns if you could, or cook me alive if that was what you had to do.'

69

His slap to the face of a dying man was brutally hard, so hard in fact that blood sprayed, a tooth flew and Smith almost lost consciousness. Ringo seized him by the throat and shook him.

'If I could do it I'd let you take a week to die you goddamn Judas!'

'They . . . they'd have killed me if I didn't take you out, Ringo. You don't know what they're like. They're the meanest bunch of bastards you ever did see . . . '

'Who are you talking about? Give me names. You owe it to me for what you did.'

A hand clutched feebly at his shirt front. By now, Osage Smith was just a grey ghost bleeding to death before his eyes. The voice was a whisper and tears ran down ruined cheeks.

'She,' he gasped weakly. 'Her . . . ' He began coughing and convulsing.

'A woman?' Ringo pressed. 'What woman? Do you mean the dancer? Don't lie. She's just a — '

'No, not her. Fay's a nothing. I just

hired her to sucker you out so's we could nail you. But you've got to understand why I did what I did, man. You ... you see, I'd lost my nerve, couldn't cut it any more. Not made of iron like you. Needed a big pay-day to retire on ... '

Smith broke off, coughing up blood now. Lots of blood. Ringo was dispassionate as he waited for him to continue.

'Give me names, not your life story.'

'The red-headed queen ... ' Smith's eyes were huge in his ashen face. 'She's worse even than he was ... Haines. But the other dame, you gotta watch her too ... they ... they ... '

'What other? Are we talking two women here?'

But Ringo's last question fell on deaf ears. He uncoiled to his feet and spat. He didn't miss.

71

3

WHITE INJUN

Waiting for his Agency contact to show, Ringo put his time to good use. Days he rode the government horse far and wide across the rolling country to the north of Fort Despair where burned-out ranches, new graves, straying cattle and Indian sign had replaced once thriving cattle kingdoms. Nights he drank very little and talked plenty around the turpentine town where he had become an overnight notoriety. Mainly what he did was ask questions when he could find someone not too scared to talk with him.

It turned out that Smith had had few friends here. Yet although the Fort Despair man in the street realized that Ringo had killed the former scout in self-defence, they were resentful that

72

Fay and her pretty can had vanished overnight after the gunplay and was believed to have left town.

Yet whatever resentment they might feel they were careful not to let it show. It was not just what Ringo had done that impressed but the manner in which he did it that scared this yellow town.

So he came and went without challenge, each hard day's work helping him flesh out the basic briefing on the Crystal Basin troubles furnished by Westerman and Carmody back at headquarters.

Agency was right when they said crime and outlawry were rife and authority virtually non-existent.

The breakdown had begun some time ago and was responsible for the once relatively peaceful Free Lands going to hell in a handbasket. The gunrunners' rifles fell into the hands of claim-jumpers, wagon-robbers, petty tyrants, Indians, rustlers and outlaws. Lawlessness and the destruction of the great ranches had led to an orgy of rustling, and greed and thievery were whipping up the flames. Conflict between the tribes and renegades both white and red had gained ascendancy in a way they had not done for years.

Citizens insisted the gunrunning had spawned the rustling plague that had struck further north like a blight, until they seemed unsure which was the greater evil. Everybody complained that 'something should be done', and he was resolved that it would.

Even apart from his assignment, he fiercely resented what was happening there and this hardened his determination to complete the assignment those cold-fish bastards back at Sweetgrass had handed him.

He figured somebody would have had to outlay big money to get his former pard to try and kill him. Maybe someone bloated and rich from gunrunning or rustling?

Standing feebly against this tide of anarchy was rundown Fort Wilson to the north-east and the Indian Agency in the heart of the basin proper on Dark River. He was told that the 6th Regiment, for which he and Osage Smith had once scouted, had declined to impotency under Colonel Patterson who was regarded as weak if well-intentioned. Indian Agent Mulvaney, on the other hand, appeared to have acquired considerable power and influence while making few friends in either Army or rancher circles.

So Ringo travelled the autumn lands familiarly but with great caution. He glimpsed the smoke of burning ranches at great distances from time to time and once came upon all that was left of some foolhardy wagoner who'd attempted to make his unescorted way up from the Powder River to the Bighorn with his wife and children, none of whom would ever get to see the Promised Land.

He knew they'd handed him a big challenge and he couldn't wait to come to grips with it.

But until that day came he would

sleep with one eye open and a gun under his pillow — and reserve his trust in the men who'd 'enlisted' him to work for Washington.

★   ★   ★

On his second day's circuit he made brief contact with a dishevelled hunting-party of Cheyenne, several of whom vaguely remembered the tow-headed skinny white kid who'd been well-known to Black Eagle's Sweet Creek tribe.

The party had no repeater Winchesters, this new rifle which had become the super weapon of plains and basin. But under persistent questioning they grudgingly revealed that some Dog Soldiers had recently come into possession of these 'wonder guns'.

He might have guessed. The Cheyenne Dog Soldier Society was as different from the regular Cheyenne tribesmen as they were from Sioux, Kiowa or Crow. The Dogs lived for war and

Winchesters were plainly the finest war weapons to be had. Even so, he knew the Dogs would have no interest in rustling. So he concentrated on questioning them on the rustlings, gunrunners, and even a white woman or women. But the Cheyenne decided they'd said enough, clammed up and went on their way. They did not want to get involved. They were hunters and fishers and wanted no part of Bluecoats, Indian wars, burning ranch houses, Dog Soldiers or a lean white scout with bristling belt guns who spoke the native tongue as fluently as they.

It was drawing on to night when the lone horseman raised the town and smelt the turpentine plant.

Apart from the fire-scarred alley and a new grave in the cemetery outside town there were few reminders of Fort Despair's night of violence to be seen now. The occasional passer-by nodded or grunted as Ringo rode down the blighted main stem. He had been in the saddle all day yet rode as straight-backed and alert as upon setting out. In truth, with his carriage and blond hair and big black-handled sixshooters bulging from tied-down holsters, he stood out sharply from Fort Despair's average citizen who came complete in unwashed denim, rounded shoulders, whiskey-reddened nose and shuffling gait — this distinction making him an easy figure to spot in the fast-fading light.

He halted in surprise when no less an individual than Carmody himself stepped down from the gallery of the Blue Angel and greeted him by name. With the Agency man was something that resembled a diseased warthog yet stood upright and dressed like a man.

* * *

Tucker clamped his big left hand over the pink body and pinned it to the wooden block while he chopped down savagely with a cowhide-hafted knife that was eighteen inches long and sharp as a razor. The head flew off with the one stroke, blood spraying wide to add to the disarray of the diner's kitchen. The big claws seemed to be still trying to remove at least one of his hairy fingers even though its soul had already fled to crawfish heaven. Tucker turned the crustacean over and slit the belly wide open, squeezing out the innards with spatulate fingers. More blood and guts.

Seated at the window table twenty feet away, Ringo arched an eyebrow at his tall companion.

'Likes seafood,' Carmody commented.

'He's a bum. How come you're travelling with the likes of him?'

'I don't care for your tone, jailbird.'

'I'm still asking.'

'All right. Tucker's with us now.'

'As what? Short order cook?'

'If you really must know he is entered on our books under the same designation as yourself. Manhunter, to use Agency parlance.'

'You are joking! He couldn't catch the plague.'

Irritation flickered across Carmody's smooth features.

'I find your preoccupation with this man quite irrelevant, Ringo. Tucker is just someone who's joined the organization, no more and no less.'

'Why are you lying?'

Carmody's eyes narrowed.

'Have a care, fellow. Your extermination of Smith here does not entitle you to special privileges or licence, let me remind you.'

'I already know how Agency works, Carmody. The fact that you arrived so soon after the shoot-up shows you've been keeping tabs on me. And why do I suspect that your bringing Tucker along has to mean you expect us to be working together, although I'm damned if I can figure why. That doesn't suit me. I'm not risking my neck riding tandem with that breed.'

Carmody turned his head to watch Tucker dump his supper into a big iron pot of boiling water. Naturally he splashed every place, the fire in the range spitting and hissing in protest. The diner's regular cook backed away to avoid the blood. Tucker was now picking his nose.

'Very well,' Carmody conceded, 'I shan't deny that your reaction is understandable. But you can relax. It's not imperative you work together. You are obviously too hostile towards the man, and now you've succeeded in making him aware of it. All right, let's get down to business. Tell me about Smith.'

Ringo related the story without embellishment or apology. Carmody heard him out as they sipped Irish coffee and waited for their steaks.

'We had some suspicion Smith might have turned his coat and gone over to the enemy. But we felt it was worth the chance of having you and him get together just in case we were wrong and he proved to be of some value. Plainly he'd sold out all the way or he wouldn't have tried to finish you.' Carmody paused, then added grudgingly: 'Er, I feel Agency should apologize for placing you in a situation where you were forced to kill a friend.'

'I don't have any friends when I'm working on a job like this. Can't afford them.' Ringo took out his tobacco. 'Want to hear what I've picked up?'

Carmody nodded and Ringo began his report. He was still talking when he finished his smoke and the food arrived. Over behind the splattered counter bench, Tucker was hauling his supper from the pot with a meat hook.

Ringo summarized his observations. Then he was guessing, yet spoke with conviction.

'You guys killed Helmut Haines the gunrunner and big-timer, right?'

'We certainly did, I'm proud to say.'

'Yet the guns kept coming. Seems to me any man that big would've had to have henchmen, people who'd want to keep such a high-paying trade going. This has got to be a line to follow when I reach the basin.'

'Naturally we thought the same way.

But, you see, Haines's main weapon was secrecy. He conducted his evil business in the basin yet did not live there. Time and time again we tried to track him to his lair, without success. Plainly he had another identity, another life. He could have been a banker from Wisconsin or holy roller from Utah. Who would know? This is the task we wanted Smith to help you with, but now it seems you'll have to go it alone.'

'I half-figured that. That's why I plan to visit Fort Wilson and find out what the army knows. Then I'll go hunt up Black Eagle. The old chief is as straight as a gun barrel and keeps his ear to the ground. I'll be looking for information on gun-running and rustling, anything I can come up with. With luck I've a hunch I can track this dead man back to home.'

Carmody actually smiled as he watched Ringo run a sharp blade through his meat.

'Once or twice I thought all the effort and expense we went to to cheat the hangman on your behalf might have been a waste, Agent Ringo. I thought it again after we got your message about what happened here. But I'm happy to advise that now once again I believe our confidence in your abilities might prove worth every cent. You are shaping up, mister. It might be prudent, however, to restrict your sixgun work where possible in the interests of — '

'You are wasting your breath,' the other cut in. 'I don't go looking for trouble but if someone makes a play, I get in first.' He swallowed some steak. 'If you hurt me, sunshine, I'll hurt you.'

The meal continued. Tucker was now consuming his crawfish at the counter, shovelling it in with his fingers and grunting. Dark-faced plant workers and sunburned cowhands watched Ringo, Carmody and Tucker in some perplexity. The trio was very different from Fort Despair's regular breed of visitor. They had already seen what Ringo was capable of and saw little that was reassuring either in the arrogant Carmody or the evil-smelling Tucker who looked like he rightly belonged in a cage.

The feeling around town was that the recent violence followed by this influx of strangers might well be linked to the troubles in some way, but nobody could be sure.

It was late when the Agency men quit the diner beneath a louring sky. A feeble slice of Plains moon was struggling to peek through, yellow and sickly. The three passed a store window in which an old framed photograph of Osage Smith had been placed on display, decorated with wild flowers.

Carmody glanced sharply at Ringo for his reaction. But Ringo was more interested in studying the cloud cover, trying to figure how tomorrow's weather would shape up for riding. Tucker shambled along behind, belching.

'How would you like to cut that racket?' Ringo snapped over his shoulder.

'How would you like to blow it out your ass, hotshot?' came the response. 'I'm up to here with you, Dingo, or whatever they call you. Button your jaw or I just might smash it off your face, show-pony.'

Ringo was ready to ruckus. This man riled him. He sensed this was mainly because Tucker was a 'dirty knifer', a breed he'd detested since childhood.

'That does it, Carmody,' he said quietly. 'I don't like his stink so I'm going to do something about it here.'

'No!' Carmody snapped. 'I forbid it.'

He might be boss yet both men ignored him.

'You're all mouth and gutwind, Ringo, standing there with two big guns bad mouthin' a man without any — '

'I'll loan you a gun if you want.'

'Tell you what, ditch the irons and I might loan you a sling to carry your Injun ass home in, squaw man.'

Guns and knives struck the street with a clatter. As the two squared off and curious heads appeared above the batwings of the nearest saloon, Carmody drew a nickel-plated pistol from a shoulder holster and brandished it, but neither man paid any attention.

There might be no logic in this set-to, yet for Ringo and Tucker it seemed inevitable as sunrise.

Ringo landed the first punch, a probing right to the forehead. Immediately Tucker dropped his ugly head and came boring in.

Ringo found himself driven back five full paces before he could halt. The knifer was strong as an ox. Ringo ripped to the guts and an elbow caromed off his cheekbone. Someone at the saloon offered odds of two to one on Tucker, which suddenly began to appear generous when the knifer connected with a right hook that landed Ringo face down and spitting dust.

He got up fast. Now he was really mad. But before another blow could land, Carmody fired two shots into the dust between their feet to bring the ruckus to a close.

'I've been lenient,' he stated, his words clearly picked up by the little crowd they'd attracted. 'Because I know I must make allowances for animals like you. But this is over now and will stay over, otherwise your commissions will be cancelled forthwith.'

He paused for a moment to afford the brawlers the opportunity of calling his bluff. Neither chose to do so, and he continued:

'You may turn in, Tucker, but you'd be advised to clean yourself up first. Ringo, you're pulling out at first light so we still have matters to discuss.'

★   ★   ★

At the Blue Angel it was the quiet end of the night, much quieter than usual due to Ringo's presence. Nubile Fay had been popular here before she got tangled up with the wrong people and was forced to decamp. Takings were down.

Carmody listened while Ringo outlined his schedule: visit Fort Wilson, contact Black Eagle, check out the Dark River Indian Agency, follow up any leads he might pick up on the way. And, of course, try to stay alive in the process. Ringo had sustained a puffed lip and a cut eyebrow in the brawl. The fight might have seemed foolish but he knew he'd needed to let off steam. They'd tried to kill him here before he'd even reached the real danger country.

'Just keep in mind the task is more important than the man,' Carmody reminded. 'I really expect you to survive this assignment, Ringo, but you should know a few things. Each time we've dispatched investigators into the Dark River region they have run into trouble, often of the fatal kind. This was why we felt we had to reach higher and went after you.' He paused. 'Why are you staring at me like that?'

'Are you worried that the spy they say has been white-anting Agency might tip the enemy off about me?'

Carmody showed no surprise that he had heard of the so-called spy. It was a common rumour associated with all intelligence units.

'There's no proof there is any spy.'

'Well, if there is we'll find out soon enough, I guess. Now, what's your estimate of the number of Winchesters coming in?'

'Tough question. But if I had to speculate I'd guess smaller rather than bigger. One shipment confiscated earlier on was just twenty weapons.'

'Just as I figured.'

'Meaning?'

'From what I've been able to scratch up, I get the hunch the gun-running has been dropping off while the rustling booms. I also hear a whisper that the runners and the rustlers have been at war lately — thieves falling out. That would account for some of the killings going on.'

Carmody stroked his clean-shaven jaw.

'That is a point that has possibly been overlooked, I'll concede.'

'Just something to think on.'

Ringo gusted smoke at the rafters

before continuing:

'Up around Savage Butte I cut a whole mess of cattle tracks and straying stock where the raiding has been worst. Seems we've got enough straying stock to mount a beef boom — if someone's found a market.'

The waitress arrived with fresh shots. She sniffed disapprovingly at Ringo as Carmody paid. Ringo was unaware; he was locked in concentration mode.

'Interesting point, Ringo,' Carmody said. 'I'll take this up with the Chief.' He nodded encouragingly. 'Any more bright ideas?'

'Women.'

'Come again?'

'Smith was babbling about women before he croaked. Seemed to be trying to tell me there were women, or at least one woman involved in his last play, maybe even involved in the bigger picture. Does Agency have any female suspects on its books out here?'

'None. And that's hardly surprising,

is it? I mean, gun-running, rustling and murder are scarcely activities one normally associates with the fair sex, are they.'

Ringo leaned back and flicked ash from his cigarette. Even relaxed he had the coiled-spring look of a resting cat.

'You are not being one hell of a lot of help, Carmody,' he stated bluntly.

'Forgive me.' Carmody's tone was ironic. 'I've been accused before of not being at my eloquent best in the company of hired butchers.'

Ringo got to his feet.

'Sure, I've had to kill in my time, Carmody. But least I'm not some bloodless bastard who sits at a desk signing chits to send real men with balls out to do what you wouldn't have the sand to do if you lived to be a thousand.'

He left.

He knew the wrangle had not settled anything. But by parting from the Agency man on bad terms he reckoned he'd headed off any last minute attempt by Carmody to change his mind and try to team him up with Tucker.

But danger and death have a way of drawing all kinds of people together, like it or not.

4

WEST OF POWDER RIVER

Grief, loss and early hardship had left no visible scars upon the face or body of the mistress of Rolling Nine ranch which lay between the Powder and Bighorn Rivers outside the town of Hudville.

Karen Rainsford of the classically featured face and superb full figure had always been a striking woman, and never more so it seemed since taking control of the biggest and most powerful ranch bordering the Free Lands.

But it was authority and not sex appeal that kept the wheels turning on the Rolling Nine.

'Your last chance, Donovan,' she snapped as she dismissed the six-foot-six horse wrangler with a wave of a gloved hand. 'One more hangover and you're through.'

'But, Miz Karen — '

'Are you still here?'

The troublemaking horseman dropped his jaw and slouched off. He'd always thought the late Buck Rainsford a tough boss but his widow made him look putty-soft.

The hand should not have been surprised. Karen Rainsford had never been a woman to take a back seat, hold her tongue or nurse disappointments and setbacks in silence as everyone from the social matrons of Hudville down to the youngest hand on the spread could testify. While business had often seen her late husband drawn away from home and hearth, particularly during the last six months of his life, Karen, now officially Widow Rainsford, ran the spread, bossed the hands, wrangled with cattle buyers and trades-men and still managed to retain her place as undisputed leader of the social upper class of lush Monroe County.

Now busy with these responsibilities she was left with no time to brood on her loss and the death in the family, which was still something of a mystery here insofar as the funeral had been held elsewhere with none of Karen and Buck's closest friends invited.

As usual the boss lady had been up and abroad before just about everybody else, and breakfast time found her taking a tray of hot cakes and coffee along to the front gallery of the sprawling Spanish-style stuccoed house which was set amongst shade trees on a grassy rise above the creek.

Stranger and Ward were not invited for breakfast, had mercly been summoned to discuss the day ahead. The two turned their heads when the boss lady appeared but neither spoke.

There was something about the Nine's top hands that Monroe County had never grown accustomed to. It was a fact that the pair could rope and brand along with the best hands on the place, if put to it. This rarely happened, and nobody was surprised. For whether she would admit it nor not, it was a fact of life on Rolling Nine that husky Stranger and lean Ward looked and acted more like Queen Karen's body-guards and troubleshooters and enforcers than regular ranch hands who knew all about drenching cattle, pitching hay and picking off the odd marauding coyote or wolf.

The pair had come to the ranch with the owners when they took over three years earlier, quickly earning a reputa-tion for arrogance and a willingness to enforce Mrs Rainsford's orders with such ruthlessness that a steady turnover in ranch personnel was inevitable.

Folks noticed that Stranger and Ward always appeared comfortable and easy in the boss lady's company, often conferred with her so long that people wondered if all the talk could be about work, or whether maybe the trio were just a bunch of rangeland gossips.

The reality of the association was so startling that few on the spread would have believed it had it ever become public knowledge.

Stranger and Ward had murder and banditry warrants posted on them in the south-west under other names and were currently actively engaged in outlawry in Wyoming Territory under the most ruthless boss they'd ever worked for, namely Karen Rainsford.

At last their business talk was concluded and Stranger relaxed and smiled for the first time today as he stretched his powerful body and inhaled the fragrances of the fall morning.

'Fine day to be riding, Miz Karen. We thought you might want us for something a tad riskier than just escorting you into town for the day. You reckon we're up to that, Eli?'

A smiling Stranger was a rare spectacle on this spread. Ward tried to imitate him but just couldn't make it. The narrow-bodied Southerner was as sour as old swill and as joyless as a eunuch's wedding-night. There were dead men who got more fun out of life than Eli Ward. But he was good at what he did and was loyal to the brand he rode for.

'Sure,' he replied in a voice as dead as last year's leaves. 'What time you want to leave, ma'am?'

'Half an hour,' Karen said, and a flick of ringed fingers sent the hard men on their way like obedient poodles.

She smiled as she watched their figures recede, reassured and excited by her power over others. She had always possessed natural authority but it had never flowered and flourished as it had in the past half-year since her husband was put in the ground.

That funeral service marked the day and the hour in which the widow and mother had emerged from backstage into the spotlight where she had blossomed like a chrysalis unfurling.

Indeed she'd taken to her new life with such gusto that occasionally this hard-driving mistress of her own affairs had to take time out and lecture herself sternly on the evils of all work and no play, for not taking time off to smell the roses.

Today was such a day. There were any number of matters clamouring for her attention, some of which would intimidate a whole board of ranch governors. But she had decided they could all wait. The sun was shining, soon full winter would be upon them, new fashions had arrived in town and she was feeling at least twenty years younger than her forty-two years.

No work today. No riding the range or conferring with accountants; no conclaving with scar-faced men bristling with guns or issuing orders the result of which might be felt clear across the great plains. Karenday, she would call it. Her day.

And her only problem — what to wear, the blue or the lavender?

She had selected the blue dress and was putting the finishing touches to her hair in the mirror when a girl with an angel face appeared in the doorway of her boudoir.

'So, you've decided on town, Mother?'

'Right, darling. Are you sure you won't come with me?'

'You know you only want me with you in the hope someone will mistake us for sisters.' This was said in a teasing tone, and both laughed. Each was beautiful and assured in her beauty, the mature woman with the hint of famished cat about her lithe quickness, the golden-ringleted girl with eyes of china blue and bee-sting lips just made for love. Two beauties without a permanent man between them, husband and father having perished under a storm of ambush lead long enough ago for them to be getting over it by now. There were those who might imply that both had recovered from their loss astonishingly well, judging by the bloom on their cheeks and the hectic social life they had followed since the tragedy.

Karen and Calla Lee knew what their enemies, the gossips, the envious and the no-account said about them. They might have been jealous and bitchy like that themselves had they been poor plain nobodies instead of the Queen and Princess Royal of Monroe County.

They strolled out through the house arm-in-arm and Calla Lee was full of tongue-in-cheek advice as poker-faced Ward handed her mother up into the gleaming rosewood-and-leather surrey.

'Never drink straight rye, Mother. Don't go dancing with any man named Ed, don't tell Reverend James what you really think about his wife and be home midnight at the latest. You mind now, hear?'

This sent Karen off in the highest of spirits, yet Calla Lee's forced gaiety had faded long before the departing rig was obliterated by the dust billowing up from rubber-tyred wheels, the driver setting a spanking pace along the town trail.

'Sure, have fun, Mother. Dance, Karen, flirt Karen, twist them around your fingers and make sure everyone knows you can snap your thumbs and get anything you want. You've earned it, so flaunt it. Trouble is, you forget we both earned it, Mother, or would like to forget it and have me forget it also . . . '

Strange sentiments coming from a loving daughter, one might think.

But what a woman didn't know couldn't hurt her and Karen's day was bright and unsullied and she leaned back against silk cushions with a Navajo blanket over silk-stockinged legs and watched the lovely scenery roll by, driver on the spring seat. Ward rode point with Stranger bringing up behind with one of the latest Winchester repeaters angled across his saddle horn.

The widow never travelled unescorted. Although this might seem like simple prudence to many, the frontier being what it was, there were some in the county who at times found it odd to see her spinning by at times with upward of half a dozen heavily armed escorts in close attendance.

Outlawry and crime were blazing across the Free Lands further west at this time, as everybody knew, yet the troubles had not infiltrated law-abiding Monroe County. Nonetheless, the mistress of Rolling Nine continued to maintain this high level of security.

Sympathetic friends claimed this was probably reaction to her husband's mysterious death. Those less charitable thought it might be simple display, just another way Karen had of reminding people that she was wealthy enough to be able to afford just as many bodyguards and servants as she wanted.

Whatever the case, this was how she liked it, and whatever Karen liked she mostly got. Today, she wanted a frilly, frivolous day with her lady friends, spending money, trying on hats, shoes and dresses, dining lavishly at Hudville's best hotel, spending the long leisurely afternoon gossiping, visiting and simply soaking up the respect and obeisance to which she felt entitled.

So it came about.

The evening was spent with three different suitors at different times, though at one stage she impishly toyed with the idea of entertaining all three simultaneously at her suite at the Bighorn Hotel, but eventually she decided against it.

The following morning in Hudville could scarcely have been more different. There had been two hard-faced businessmen from Montana awaiting an audience with Karen for several days, and today she granted it. With Stranger and Ward standing guard on the locked doors of the hotel's conference room, the range mistress talked business and planned operations with her South Dakota associates for four hours straight. After the dealers had quit and headed east she allowed the two weary gunmen to guide their mistress home, where she found everything much as she had left it other than that her daughter had 'gone drifting' again.

Calla Lee had developed the habit of simply saddling up and vanishing, sometimes just for a few hours but at others going for days, a week. Karen was naturally curious yet hardly concerned. She was one of the few people who understood her daughter thoroughly and as a consequence entertained few fears for her safety. If any girl could look after herself it was that one.

She slept the day away while hard-working riders criss-crossed the ranch making her wealthier, simple cowhands eternally herding cattle and working for the Karendollar. Others worked for the same, such as the two men she had conclaved with in town, owners of a rapidly expanding meat-packing company in Montana.

Karen slept so well because so very few knew her secrets. It disturbed her sometimes to suspect her daughter might have her own secrets also, but she was comforted by the belief that even if this were the case, Calla Lee's little secrets could never be anywhere near as dark, ambitious and spine-chillingly risky as her own.

★   ★   ★

This was the real prairie and deep in the heart of the trouble country known as the Free Lands.

The government cayuse picked up the weary rhythm of its shuffling gait as the rider's gaze quartered his gloomy surrounds. Eventually Ringo relaxed and ran his hand up and down the horse's sweating neck.

'I said we'd make it by nightfall, Gov. And there it is, Dark River, wide as a squaw's bottom and twice as welcome. We'll raise the fort by moonset sure as shooting now. Army chow for me, weevilly grain for you — and maybe our gun-runners served up to us on a platter. What do you figure?'

They said talking to your horse was a bad sign. Ringo didn't see it that way. It was a lifelong habit. With a horse, you could reveal all your secrets, plans and uncertainties and they never went any further. He liked that. With people, the next human being he confided in completely would be his first. That was the Indian influence in his makeup, he liked to think. Cut down on the talk and always get in with the first punch. Laws for loners to live by.

Ahead lay Dark River upon which both the Indian Agency and Fort Wilson stood, although many miles apart. This fording lay upriver from Fort Wilson where willows shimmered mysteriously in the night wind and little fish made breathrings on the waters. A few stars were out lending the surface a ghostly starwash. This was their first whiff of water since daybreak. Summer on the great plains had been hot and dry, the first fall rains were yet to come. Nostrils belling gratefully, the horse lifted its flagging gait.

Ringo watered and curried the horse before tending his own needs. Tonight it would be sourdough biscuits and jerky. No coffee, no fire, no risk-taking of any kind. The Free Lands was hostile country now, gun-runner country, rustler country. A man would never run short of danger out here.

He ate sparingly and washed it down

with cool river water. Seated on a deadfall where he could see in all directions, he made a long, intense survey of the riverland before taking out pipe, tobacco and pocket flint. Days he smoked cigarettes and cigars but at night the pipe came out. The Cheyenne never smoked during the day, storing up the pleasure of the pipe for night. In looking back, he'd only spent a short time with the Indians, while his painterly folks were off someplace searching for the perfect sunset; there were many things he still did that were picked up from them. He took his time packing the bowl with shagcut, eyes never still.

During the day he had cut a deal of sign, some of which he found curious. Midday buzzards drew him to a draw where two beeves injured in a stampede had perished. The survivors had run, or were driven, east. Seemed gun-runners, troopers, renegades and miscellaneous Plains travellers criss-crossed every which way, yet in the main the cattle tracks always angled away north-east.

Curious that. To the east lay Monroe County, peaceful and prosperous. There was no rustling activity on the peaceful side of the Big Horns that he knew of. Due north was Montana Territory.

Eventually he was reassured enough to set fire to his tobacco and settled down for a half-hour smoke. Suddenly he knocked the dead dottle from the pipe and rose as silently and smoothly as a six-foot cat.

The horse greeted him with a whicker. Ringo slipped his hand beneath loosened cinch and saddle blanket to ensure that the gelding was properly cooled out. In his time he had seen more men come to grief through careless use of horseflesh than from all the bushwhackers' bullets or feather-tipped arrows in the West. Cinching up, it took but a minute to ready for the trail again. He filled leather and started off, loping westwards along the watercourse, man and horse forming a shadowy part of the night, hoofbeats muffled in the short thick grass. Suddenly he reined in and stared: *What the hell . . . ?*

The cause of his puzzlement was the bright glow of a night fire maybe two miles downstream towards the fort. His eyesight might be twenty-twenty, but that still wasn't good enough to be able to tell whether there was anyone round that blaze. But if there was, so he reasoned, it had to be someone without a wheel in his thinkbox. Be it white man, Indian or in-between, it didn't matter. Anyone who would light up a fire like that in a region where not even the Army had been able to maintain peace in almost a year must be loco, suicidal or perhaps out of their skulls on something like a glazed jug of Taos Lightning.

The last guess proved to be virtually dead on target.

Where the bushel-sized blaze of the camp-fire blossomed so cheerily on the south banks of the Dark and lit up the river for a hundred yards in either direction, five figures squatted in its welcoming warmth. In the background the firelight ruddily touched a high-sided Army freighter loaded up with stove wood and hooked on to three span of weary mules.

The firewood detail from Wilson had been overtaken by darkness and had decided to make camp until moonrise; they got a fire going and broke out the rum ration to ward off the sharp chill in this basin night.

The happy troopers had passed the tall-tales stage of inebriation and were working on some grating three-part harmony when the shadowy figure appeared suddenly in the fireglow.

The singing stopped abruptly.

Slowly the figure took the form of a trim-muscled man around six feet tall in a hip-length buckskin shirt and sporting twin Colts.

The sudden appearance dried the harmony up in their throats and they stared round at their rifles, neatly stacked in a pyramid — but fifty feet distant. Then they all began babbling at once in a way that confirmed beyond doubt what Ringo had already strongly suspected. These were boot troops. Greeners. No training, no discipline and not a sober brain amongst the five of them. Without a word he came forward disgustedly to kick the fire apart, scattering sticks and coals every which way across the sand. Only then did he speak.

'Jesse Ringo, heading in to see the colonel . . . ' he advised, jaundiced gaze playing over them. 'Although looking at you I wonder if a man should bother . . . '

He was implying that if the rank and file were so undisciplined and foolhardy then the disease must be rampant behind the sun-dried walls of Fort Wilson. So it proved to be.

Colonel Patterson, for whom he and Osage Smith had once scouted, had fallen victim to isolation, insurrection, administrative indifference, bitterness, failure and eventually but possibly inevitably, the demon drink.

The commander was ridiculously happy to see his stalwart former First Scout Jesse Ringo again, and for a brief moment was fired by the hope he'd come back after so long to volunteer his specialized services. When he realized this was not the case, Colonel Patterson all but begged him to stay on. It might have been flattering to have a high-ranking officer regard you in such a light, but Ringo did not see it that way. He was embarrassed, as he had genuinely admired Patterson and was disgusted to see what time and adversity had done to the man.

He was hardly surprised to have Patterson review the prevailing situation as 'just one big, confusing, bloody mystery'. The man plainly had no worthwhile information to impart. Ringo soon excused himself on a pretext and got on his horse. As he signalled to the gate sentry and rode swiftly away, he looked back. He slotted the weak-kneed soldier as just another victim of the mystery of the great plains. Which an outfit called Agency was expecting one man to solve.

Leads led no-place, authority was crumbling, men died, cattle vanished and even Agency was reduced to relying on one or two men to draw their irons out of the fire.

His thoughts touched momentarily on Tucker. He sniffed, as though he could smell him. Tucker was out here someplace, he knew. He sensed the man was irritated because he was too much like Jesse Ringo. Solitary, driven, dangerous.

He shook his head.

Forget Tucker and do your job, loner. Get it done and never think of quitting. He never quit a thing once started, and this time he couldn't, being free but not officially pardoned.

Immediately he felt resolute, the self-discipline he'd learned from Black Eagle standing by him again. Ever since, once started in on a thing he just kept pushing, shoving, butting and swinging until something gave.

He stopped over for an overnight visit with Black Eagle at Sweet Creek. The chief was full of charm and affection but no information, no inside knowledge about gun-runners or rustlers. In a way Ringo was relieved that the village plainly had no involvement with the troubles. Let them hunt and fish and gather their wild rice, and allow others to fret about guns and cattle and killing. Others like him.

He spent the day at the village then set out by darkness from Sweet Creek to cut eastwards across country for the Dark River Indian Agency to visit with agent Mulvaney.

But Mulvaney, the man who had proved himself capable of prospering where predecessors had failed, was absent, nobody appeared to know where or why. He waited for dark again — no man with any serious interest in staying alive would ride about this region alone by daylight these days when you never knew what look-out might be watching you through murderous eyes.

But the Indian Agency visit was not a complete waste of time. From that station, Ringo journeyed east for Mirror Lake west of the Little Big Horn River on the strength of nothing more than something a drunk teamster had slurred to him over whiskeys at the bar. Something about mysterious cattle tracks where none should rightly be.

5

DRYGULCH GUNS

'What in Hades sort of coffee do they call this?' grouched Westerman.

'Straight without whiskey in it, Chief,' murmured Carmody, still studying the message just delivered from Communications down the corridor.

'Why no whiskey?'

Carmody glanced up. It was unusual for Westerman to be this testy.

'You rarely take liquor this early, Chief,' he reminded. Unlike his superior Carmody appeared untroubled by Agent Ringo's puzzling wire from the north.

There was ice in the veins of the second-in-command of Agency, a quality his superior often envied. Both men were ruthless, but while Westerman had the power, his deputy had the cool head

— most times, leastways.

The pair's value to Washington and the Wyoming legislature was that they got things done without anybody showing too much interest in how they managed consistently to achieve their high success rate.

'Maybe it's because I'm beginning to seriously doubt the wisdom of your insistence on recruiting that jailbird, Carmody. Prise a killer out of the Death House to fill the shoes of a highly trained operator then send him off on a jigsaw assignment that has baffled us for months! I must have been crazy to listen to you. Get me some whiskey to put in this coffee, mister!'

Unprotesting, Carmody produced a bottle from a polished cabinet, measured out two fingers, poured them smoothly into the steaming pannikin. Westerman gulped and cursed. Too strong. But Carmody still did not react. He had bigger things on his mind.

'I don't agree any error has been

made. In this message he has merely — '

'Why the devil isn't he concentrating on the gun-runners? Doesn't he know the whole bloody mess in the Free Lands began with guns? That is what that gallows-cheater is supposed to working on.'

'And is.' Carmody sounded as though he was tolerating the older man. 'But he appears to have uncovered sign around Mirror Lake indicating prolonged usage of the area to round up cattle stock that has been running wild due to the range war.'

He tapped the pink telegraph slip.

'Seems more and more that rustling is what we should be focusing on.' When this drew no response, he continued: 'Care to take a look at this, Chief?'

The map he'd unrolled and weighted down on a large table was of the Big Horn Mountains region at the far north of the Free Lands whence Ringo's latest communication had issued.

'This is not all that far from the

Montana border if rustlers wanted to drive the herds out of Wyoming, Chief.' His finger swept right. 'Or South Dakota if they had a market there. And beef prices have been booming, which would surely give extra incentive to anybody involved in cattle-thieving on the grand scale.'

'Are you now saying Haines was a rustler and not a gun-runner, mister?'

'Well, I know for a fact that that slippery customer was a gun-runner. But surely a successful criminal could be both?'

Another silence.

The uncovering and execution of Haines — a bad man believed to have lived a double life — had been a feather in Agency's cap. But the fact that outlawry had blossomed in the Free Lands since the death of their top Free Lands operative Bickner was certainly a black mark.

Now it seemed their new man was giving them problems and questions instead of the quick results they craved.

Westerman stared at Carmody who

remained by the map table against a backdrop of the northern hills. At last he sighed and drained his mug.

'Very well. Advise him we'll consider his theory and are prepared to offer whatever support he might need to follow his rustling theory through. Only get it goddamn done fast! Identify the crime and the king pin, then eliminate him. Make it clear what is expected of him.'

Carmody smiled. He loved the clean, antiseptic clarity and finality of the word 'eliminate'. It was the principal reason he chose to work for Agency and why he derived such satisfaction from working with other dangerous men, such as Ringo.

'I'll get a message off to him immediately, Chief,' he said, going out. 'He gave Whitefoot as his next contact point.'

* * *

It was a long time since he'd ridden the old outlaw trail but Jesse Ringo was feeling anything but nostalgic as he stepped down to allow his horse to drink at the stream. Then he stepped back to stretch tight shoulders and aching back. Three days of almost unbroken riding and more than a hundred hard miles covered, but worth it every one.

For right now in this wind-blowing night in the rugged hills separating the Free Lands from plush Monroe County, he was still following the sign he'd picked up in Stone Canyon thirty miles north-west at the huge rustlers' rendezvous on the Montana side of the border.

He owed his 'lucky' strike at Stone Canyon to one Jubal Priest, his former teak-tough partner in the toughest job of all, guiding greenhorn Easterners across Wyoming and over the snowy Divide to the promised land of Utah.

Nobody knew the Free Lands like Jubal Priest. And though the man hadn't known who was behind the rustling, he was able to affirm the trade was far bigger even than Ringo figured.

He told him about the railhead up in Montana that accepted the stolen stock and rolled it East, and the fact that the big gangs used the old outlaw trail to run their stolen beeves from the cattle lands to the border and beyond.

The horse lifted its weary head, water running from its jaws. Man and beast were all played out but that didn't stop Ringo throwing a leg across and banging heels on horsehide.

'I figure about another ten miles and we'll hit rangeland, Gov,' he muttered, stifling a yawn. There was no way he was going to quit this hoof-ripped trail of some fifteen to twenty cow-thieves until they led led him to their lair.

Or so he reckoned at that time.

He'd covered less than three miles of rough going before reining in abruptly. At this spot, below a massive elm, three riders had branched off from the gang and changed direction sharply.

Ringo knew exactly where he was. The three were following a little used goat-track trail climbing away in the direction of Monroe County's south-ernmost valley, Whitefoot.

Why?

He sat his saddle for five minutes puzzling on that, his curiosity piqued. He'd never considered the county in any way involved with the rustling. On a hunch he tilted his hatbrim low and followed the sign.

★　★　★

He calculated he'd covered less than two miles before it happened. He had no warning and no hint of danger. This might have been due to a drygulcher's skills, or more likely to the simple fact that Jesse Ringo had crossed the dividing line between exhaustion and alertness hours before.

The shot erupted from an innocent-looking ridge crest off to his right a split second following the searing pain that raked his left forearm.

The horse immediately broke into a gallop and Ringo urged it on with a savage cut of spur when two further shots howled so close there could be no doubting he was up against a marksman.

There was a stand of trees directly ahead. He headed for it at full gallop, ducking and weaving as the gunfire continued. The trees loomed. Kicking loose of the stirrups he hurled himself from the saddle and rolled violently several times before throwing his body between two sturdy trunks where he lay motionless with the echo of the shots still pounding in his ears, breath tearing at his lungs.

He'd come close to death before and that had been close.

The sound of shooting was replaced by hoofbeats.

This wasn't good.

The way he figured, a solitary sniper would wait longer to find out if he was dead or merely wounded. But that rumbling drumroll of approaching hoof-beats warned he was dealing with superior numbers with confidence in their strength.

The trio he'd been tailing — if he had any guess.

Yet he was cool as he lay in his bed of leaves with sleepy little birds chirruping in alarm from a brushy draw close by. Times like this he reverted to pure warrior. This had given him the edge in many a life-or-death showdown and he was calling on it again.

He thumbed back his rifle hammer and assessed his position. He had reasonable cover, two sixshooters, a rifle, a hole in his arm and a good supply of tobacco should this turn into a siege situation. He'd been worse off than this.

They came on swiftly across a leaf-littered slope, three lean shapes, guns glittering, fanning out as they approached gun range. They were yipping and yelling to one another. Excited at the prospect of a kill.

Outlaws.

There could be no mistake. The mark of the owlhoot was upon all three, exactly as he'd expected. From the moment that slug bit his arm he guessed he was up against pros, and this trio looked the part each one.

They jeered and tried to tempt him to show himself as they circled the stand, searching for a way to come in on him from behind cover. They didn't find it. Ringo hadn't had time to consider defence capability when he'd head-dived into the trees, but it made him feel better to realize now that there was open ground encircling the trees.

Angry and impatient, the attackers now reined in and loosed a thunderous volley while he lay motionless listening to steel-jacketed slugs slam into tree trunks and shake down more leaves. A ricochet ripped off the heel of his boot but he didn't move a muscle.

A whole Winchester load of lead whined and slapped about him. A pistol shot sounded its sharp angry note and lead plucked down a branch fifteen feet distant.

He smiled grimly, face pressed into the grass. They were pros but were too damned anxious. Then — there, off to the left.

The horseman had wound up his horse lower down so that when his head and shoulders appeared above the slope of the knoll he was travelling at top speed and shooting fast and straight.

But the Agency man had him squarely in his sights.

He squeezed trigger. A tongue of flame belched orange-red, lifted the rider's hat and drove it way back. The man's body was curving in agony until Ringo's next bullet smashed him out of his saddle to leave the horse running free and wild-eyed in terror.

A dead man stared at the sky and the knoll was suddenly quiet. It stayed that way but Ringo didn't move.

They would soon tire of this. Would have to make a decision to come check him out up close and personal or simply decide he was finished and ride on.

It was several uncertain minutes before he heard them coming.

Ringo licked his lips and rolled over

smoothly with the rifle snugged into his shoulder. The pair were spread wide. But that would not save them. His lip curled in contempt. Not good enough to do the job properly in the first place, now not smart enough to admit they'd fouled up and just leave it lie at that. The barrel-chested towhead on the dun gelding took a bullet somewhere but it wasn't a stopping shot.

Immediately the other began shouting and shooting. Ringo was forced to expose himself a little to draw a bead on the ugly runt astride a brown broomtail. Ragged and shrill through the reverberating crash of his rifle came the scream and through the smoke he saw his man pitch forward from the saddle on to his head to be engulfed by the grass.

Ringo dropped low.

He grimaced as pain grabbed his wounded arm. He didn't react as a bullet from the husky towhead smacked close, but the second unexpected shot drove him flat again as he sensed more than saw the powerful figure leap to ground.

'You're a dead man, snooper!' The shout was louder than a gunshot. 'I'm gonna kill you where you set!'

He realized the dry-gulcher would be momentarily vulnerable as he headed for tree cover. He didn't hesitate. He simply assessed the situation, leapt erect and charged, firing as he went.

A startled face gaped at him from between two canting trees. The man ducked and Ringo came on through the powder smoke, triggering furiously. Two bullets took the man in the chest and catapulted him backwards, sixgun going one way, Stetson hat another.

Sprawled on his back the ambusher stared at the sky in puzzlement that it could be so dark at noon. His life ran away on a black tide.

A leaf fluttered past Ringo's face in the sudden brutal quiet.

'Never make promises you can't keep, scum.'

6

CONSPIRATORS

Vista was a sober and sizable valley town where the law was respected and seemed aloof and distant from the rumours of ongoing outlawry and terror drifting in from the Free Lands to the west. This wealthy corner of the Territory enjoyed relative peace and prosperity and tended to disparage those regions that could not or did not wish to aspire to the same level of civilized living.

There was even a theatre in Vista where plays and musicals were shown each weekend. The place boasted a sheriff and two deputies, enjoyed close social and commercial contacts with Hudville to the south and even nursed ambitions of attracting the railroad down from Montana within the next year or two.

The place was also large enough to sustain two doctors, one of whom warned Ringo there was some bone damage to his wounded arm which would require rest and ongoing dressing to ensure against infection.

This was the junior of the two medicos, a seedy fellow with cigarette ash on his vest, who happily accepted twenty dollars in return for not making the presence of a stranger with a fresh bullet wound in his arm common knowledge. Ringo paid his twenty bucks readily but felt obliged to back it up with a veiled threat of what could happen should the man renege on their agreement. Ringo was here to get patched up and wire his report back. Nothing more.

He was resting up late the following day when word reached town of the discovery of three dead men fifteen miles north. He watched and waited for the jailhouse's reaction, but there was none. He found this puzzling but attributed it to something as simple as civic pride. Vista was a town going places. Why raise a fuss over an incident that could only bring the place into disrepute. The shootings, gun-running and rustling belonged to that violent, low-grade sector of the Free Lands across the Pinegrove Range, surely. It seemed that valley folk minded their own affairs and considered the troubles of other places none of their concern.

Which suited Ringo just fine as he had his dressings changed again, collected a wire from Agency, sampled the valley whiskey and enjoyed both the rest and the fine accommodations at the Alliance Hotel. He wanted no fuss about the killings, no threatening investigations.

In his mind now he was convinced that the men he'd encountered had been the top hands in the gang; they'd broken away to ride deliberately into Monroe County, which in turn told him that, whoever they were, they'd been heading to base at the end of a lengthy trail drive to Montana.

He meant to spend a little time here, keep sharp and maybe get a line on just where the ambushers had been heading when he caught up with them.

He planned to return to full duty as soon as he was fit enough.

He sensed no hint or forewarning of something unexpected and dangerous heading his way fast.

★   ★   ★

'Most everyone agreed that the mysterious girl known in Vista only as Miss Lee could snare 'most any man she set her sights on, which made it all the more difficult to figure why she should seem so smitten with a man like Jed Mulvaney.

Not that there seemed much wrong with the Indian Agent from Dark River, at least at first glance. Plainly this husky, arrogant fellow with the iron jaw and brusque manner was successful in his field, obviously earned a good income and appeared besotted by his stunning blonde companion whom he met occasionally here in the valley town.

It was Mulvaney's overbearing manner, his general unpopularity and mysterious and unexplained comings and goings which encouraged people to feel the pretty girl might do better. There were any number of eligible bachelors here who would give their eye teeth for a date with Mulvaney's girl if only she would give them a tumble.

But she didn't. The big romance — which apparently had begun several months earlier, appeared to be strong as ever that weekend as the couple was to be seen strolling hand in hand, dining at the best spots and cosying up together at the Valley Hotel.

But why did they choose Vista for their trysts? Who was she anyway — really? And what was the story on the strangers the lovers entertained from time to time, mean, wild-looking fellows who came, visited with the couple some then left again without anyone learning their names, their business or what brought them here?

'One thing's for sure,' opined the no-nonsense sheriff on the trio's most recent visit, 'that type sure don't belong this side of the range.'

Nobody disagreed. Always aloof and superior, the county had grown even more so as the Free Lands sank deeper and deeper into crime and violence, boosting their law forces and discouraging outsiders. They mightn't like the look of the couple's occasional visitors. But they never stayed, and besides, the girl's charm and attractiveness seemed to compensate. They liked the fact that their town seemed to suit the two to a T, and folks guessed they'd go on coming here until they either fell out or decided to make it permanent.

That was Vista's attitude and it suited Calla Lee Rainsford and Mulvaney just fine on their current visit as they strolled the streets, talked long and intensely over their late suppers and avoided close contact with the citizenry in the way they'd done from the outset.

Until the deaths of three men twenty miles away up in the wild country jolted the lovers for reasons they were unable to reveal. This bloody incident was followed just twenty-four hours later by their receipt of a coded wire from Sweetgrass by a spy on Mulvaney's retainer who was employed as a clerk at a place simply named Agency.

Amongst other information of a classified nature contained in the wire was a description of the latest addition to Agency's handful of lethal field men. Next day a badly shaken Calla Lee Rainsford took especial care with her hair and wardrobe before venturing abroad alone for a promenade along the main street which eventually led her to the solid brick-and-stone one-storey hotel named the Alliance, where she stopped off for mid-morning coffee at the diner. And lingered.

★　★　★

Sleep until noon. Why not? After all, Agency had ordered him to stay put and recuperate while they decided what steps should be taken following the shoot-out. He was unwinding after a pretty rugged and dangerous week, but convinced his assignment was at last beginning to look to be leading someplace.

What better time to take it easy.

For one thing was crystal-clear now, accepted by both himself and Agency. Although gun-running had initiated the wave of outlawry in the Free Lands, broken up the ranches and set thousands of cattle adrift, rustling had plainly taken over and was earning someone a fortune.

How entrenched and ruthless this operation really was had been made clear by his visit to Stone Canyon, the backtracking of the rustlers and probably most convincingly, by the attempt upon his life by gunmen posted along the side track of the outlaw trail.

As he saw it, this indicated that when

Agency decided he was fit to saddle up again there should be action aplenty. A rustling operation this size required a mess of men to run it, likely even more numbers than one man could rightly expect to handle. Besides which he had other tips from Jubal that would bear following up.

So he stored up his strength, loafed until midday, then shaved, bathed in the big tub room in back, dressed in freshly laundered rig and headed through the lobby to start his day as he had done the previous two, with coffee at the diner.

She was seated alone at a table by the window gazing dreamily out over the street. Naturally she was the customer he noticed first. A man would need to be six feet under not to react to anyone who looked the way she did, with her hour-glass figure set off by a beautifully tailored gown and golden ringlets tumbling around an angel face.

The picture she created gave Jesse Ringo a pleasurable jolt, he wouldn't deny it. Yet he remained outwardly casual as he threaded his way through to a table by the servery to take his seat and place his hat upon the chair beside him. Men like him simply did not appeal to women like that who radiated quality and breeding just as strongly as he knew he radiated danger. That was reality number one. Number two was that women were definitely not on the agenda of Agent Ringo on this valley stopover even if she was his type — the sweet and sexy type, that was.

So he ordered hot and black from the bouncy waitress with the pearly teeth and was rolling his first cigarette of this late-starting day when he glanced up to see her smiling across the room at him. Not the waitress, who was most probably more his type, but the blonde angel.

Although aware of the effect he could have upon a certain kind of female, Ringo still shot a quick glance over his shoulder to make sure no handsome, well-dressed and visibly upperclass gentleman was seated somewhere directly in back of him.

There wasn't.

He stared directly at the girl and tapped his chest. Me? She nodded shyly and whatever it was that he'd been thinking about as he rolled his smoke was forgotten in an instant, leaving his mind pleasantly blank as he collected his hat and crossed to her table.

'Morning, Miss. Care for some company?'

'I hope you won't think me too forward, but I just hate sitting alone.'

That was where it began. She told him her name was Calla Lee and he gave his real name, for what could the name Jesse Ringo mean to a girl like this? Over drinks she revealed she lived on a ranch with her mother down South, along with lots more about herself, before insisting she show him around the town. She was sympathetic about his arm, which he said had been hurt in a fall, and she didn't seem aware of the afternoon hours drifting pleasantly by.

He was both impressed and intrigued.

But he was still Ringo, which meant he remained wary despite the temptation to give himself over fully to the pleasure of the moment and just let the good times roll.

He reckoned she had to be up to something.

He'd spent too much of his life in rough company not to be eternally suspicious.

Everything about this one spoke of class. She told him she was wealthy, and he believed it. Claimed she did not have any suitors, which he found hard to swallow. Explained she was taking a brief vacation in the valley and seemed genuinely interested in finding out just who he was and what he did for a living.

He was vague in response, advising that he dealt in horses and occasionally cattle. She in turn informed that she had lost her father two years earlier, that she liked children, was only vaguely interested in men but thought he was 'interestingly different', as she phrased it with a smile. On parting at dusk she asked shyly if they might take coffee again in the morning.

Ringo watched her walk away from him and imagined he could actually feel some of the suspicion leeching out of his veins. Maybe she was genuine. Maybe he had lucked upon a high-grade woman who was genuinely interested in taking a walk on the wild side. Stranger things had happened. He knew for sure he'd be in the hotel diner next morning. Early.

He visited his doctor, then checked at the telegraph office. The coded message from Agency was virtually a repeat of the one previous: recuperate and maintain contact.

He retired early after a couple of shots but didn't sleep. He had no trouble figuring out why.

* * *

Calla Lee glanced up from her supper at the sound of his step on the stair. There was no mistaking it. Mulvaney weighed more than 200 pounds and walked with purpose, like he did everything else.

He came in soberly and pitched his hat at the sofa. The Indian Agent had an Irish name but looked Prussian with close-cropped hair, lantern jaw and a humourless expression. He had secured his posting at Dark River simply because he out-impressed the other candidates. He ran the agency with an iron hand and there were few complaints about the way he discharged his duties. He seemed to have a knack for handling Indians from a position of authority and dealt with other problems firmly and effectively.

Of course there was always talk about men in such positions, and his detractors variously labelled Mulvaney as secretive, ambitious and arrogant to a fault. There were also complaints about his frequent absences from Dark River which several times had landed him in hot water with the Bureau of Indian Affairs. Apart from this, his position seemed secure enough, which was remarkable considering the real reason Jed Mulvaney had come to the Free Lands.

He dropped heavily into a chair and Calla Lee rose to pour him a drink. Her manner was subservient and anxious, quite different from when they appeared in public.

'Well?' she enquired.

'I tagged him after he left you,' the man stated. 'He visited that quack on Fletch Street. I checked with the croaker and he told me this Ringo hurt his arm in a fall — just like he told you. But when I flashed cash he admitted he's treating him for a bullet wound.'

'I see.' Calla Lee sat down slowly. 'Then that clinches it. He must be the one who killed Toogood, Goldman and Crackshawl.'

The big man nodded grimly.

'We were pretty sure of that after getting that wire from Burke in Sweetgrass. But this puts it beyond doubt. He's the Agency man, he's here, and he's getting hot. How do you size him up?'

Calla Lee rose swiftly to pace the room, fingering the elegant gold ring on her right hand, her fine brows cut hard in concentration.

'The moment I laid eyes on him I could tell why Agency hired him. He's very attractive and quite charming company, but you can sense the wolf in him. The colour of his eyes and the way he moves. You could picture him roving alone over the high plains, seeing everything, reading the signs . . . just like an Indian. Or how he might be ambushed by three men yet still put them all in their graves.'

She paused momentarily and rubbed her arms as though cold.

'I don't believe I've ever met a more dangerous man.'

'That's a big statement to make considering some of the people we have working for us. Both Karen and me, I mean.'

The girl's face was blank. She lived in

147

terror. This man was part of it. She continued in a toneless voice.

'Ringo must be awaiting further orders from Agency. These could arrive at any moment and he could be gone; where, we would not know.'

'We can't risk that. This gunner is a loose cannon. Maybe he's a job that your mother should take on. She's got men at her disposal on the spread, while I'm still waiting for mine to get back from Montana. Sure, let Karen handle it. She's good at taking care of people . . . right?'

Calla Lee's face shadowed and for just a moment her eyes on the man's hard face were cold and distant.

'She is not the only one whom that cap fits, Jed.'

'Meaning me?'

'Forget it.' She gazed moodily from the window a moment. 'But I do believe you are right. Mother should be the one to deal with this . . . ' She turned slowly. 'If I can persuade Ringo to come visit with us, that is.'

'You can persuade most any man do most any damn thing.'

'I still feel uneasy. It would feel like taking a wolf into our home . . . '

Mulvaney's look was icy.

'So? It will be Karen dealing with the wolf, not you or me . . . '

She caught on to his meaning.

'Of course — mother dearest. She is used to taking risks. Me? I'll just stand back and look all sweet and innocent. As usual.'

He took her into his powerful arms.

'And nobody does that better.' He kissed her. 'When will you go see him?'

'It had better be tonight.'

'What if he won't agree?'

Calla Lee unbuttoned the top of her dress.

'Then I'll just have to persuade him, won't I?'

★   ★   ★

Through the chilly grey of the fog-patched morning the Storm River fording emerged as drear and desolate as the devil's dooryard. The river's clay banks were eroded sharply here where it curved through dun-colored hills. The icy rain, a misting drizzle since they'd set out from the valley, abruptly thinned out then stopped, leaving river, trees and hills seeming to float in a ground smoke of drifting fog.

The water only came up to the horses' bellies and by the time they were cutting south again there was a hint of sunlight over the eastern river bluffs.

Ringo's arm was aching some, which he welcomed. For the wound was the excuse he was making for quitting Vista and heading south away from the rustlers' trail and his duty. He doubted Agency would accept the excuse of his injury; there could even be swift reaction from Westerman and Carmody when they got his wire outlining his movements.

The big question was — was he letting Agency down or simply doing the job they'd hired him to do?

He planned to inform Agency he'd been approached by a woman in such an unlikely way that he was prompted to go along with her in the hope she might turn out to have some sort of link with the rustlers.

He just couldn't believe a girl of her class could be genuinely interested in a man like himself. The girl had revealed that morning that home was the Rolling Nine ranch, a major cattle outfit operated by powerful people. The outfit was run by a woman, Calla Lee's mother, and he recalled Jubal Priest say it was a ball-breaker outfit, whatever that meant.

But how much was he driven by duty and how much by the reality that she was young, beautiful, high-class and at least didn't seem scared off by him?

He glanced at her and she smiled, causing him to look away.

He was just doing his job, he had to remind himself — yet again. And naturally he would remain as suspicious as a once-trapped dog wolf confronted by a slab of prime buffalo steak turning up at the mouth of his den, and maybe, just maybe she might lead him to the cattle-thieves.

For underlying every other reason he was dredging up to validate his decision to accept her invitation was that the track from the outlaw trail he'd followed up over the hump of Pinegrove Range ran directly towards the sprawl of the Rolling Nine ranch.

Then an inner voice whispered: 'Who are you trying to kid, Ringo? You know she ain't mixed up with anything crooked. If she wasn't so pretty would you be letting her waltz you home to see the folks in the middle of a dangerous job? She's suckered you in. She's pure class; you're ripe for something great in your life after Ellison. If you'd turned her down and let her just slip away you might regret it the rest of your life.' And the clincher: 'You're only working for Agency, they don't own you.'

He shook his head and got totally serious now. Just say she wasn't innocent. What if he found she was indeed part of the rustlers' empire? Would he be able to kill her?

The longer he'd sat yarning with Jubal the more he learned about such badmen as company crooks, mine-salters, confidence tricksters and out and out desperadoes who'd attracted the attention of outside investigations and wound up gunned down like dogs — the more he believed that Agency was in fact an extermination unit.

Which made him a potential exterminator!

He was sure he couldn't be that cold-blooded. But what was the alternative? Back to Ellison facing the rope for a second time?

He shook his head and told himself to quit thinking and just go with his instincts. The day was fresh with the sun struggling through mist and it was good just to let rough gaited Gov carry him on south in her company and savour the moment. It was almost as though he wanted this image they must present — young man and lovely woman travelling happily and innocently together — to turn out to be true, innocent and clean.

So what if his life had never been that way. Things could change, couldn't they? But when reality intruded he scowled and fingered his arm. And wondered if this could be two-gun Ringo thinking this mushy way or if his bullet wound was making him feverish.

7

DEADLIER THAN THE MALE

Ringo stared at Karen Rainsford's thick, shoulder-length hair. It was a deep and lustrous shade of red which was strikingly unusual, and instantly set his memory clicking back to a man dying in agony on a Fort Despair street, struggling desperately to reveal something about an evil woman with vivid red hair . . .

He shook his head. That was loco thinking. Calla Lee's mother radiated wealth, privilege, class and then some. And Monroe County could be full of redheads with husky voices for all he knew.

He suddenly realized the woman was staring at him, her expression quizzical.

'Pardon, Jesse,' she said, 'but is there something wrong with my appearance, perhaps? You were staring so . . . ?

He sharpened up smartly to take the woman's hand in response to her daughter's introduction, lifted it to his lips. It was rare indeed that he he got to play the gentleman, the circles he moved in.

'Sorry, ma'am. I guess I was staring,' he smiled. 'I reckon the shock of meeting two beautiful women in the same family took me by surprise. It's a pleasure to make your acquaintance, Mrs Rainsford.'

'Karen, please. And it's always a pleasure to meet my daughter's friends, even at such short notice.'

'I was sure you wouldn't mind, Mother,' smiled Calla Lee.

'Of course not, darling . . . '

The mother was studying Ringo again with a frown as if trying to recall something. He wasn't surprised when she snapped her fingers and remembered what it was.

'Ringo! I wondered why that name sounded familiar. The newspapers . . . '

She broke off, one hand to her bosom. 'Oh, but of course there wouldn't be any connection between you and that . . . that awful person they — '

'That they were aiming to hang?' he finished for her. He nodded, cool and easy. 'Uh huh, that was me as a matter of fact. But I guess you read the papers after as well as before? Hitch in the legal system, they called it. I told them they had the wrong man and they wound up believing it.' He nodded to the girl. 'I meant to tell you but didn't get round to it. If this makes any difference . . . ?'

'Of course not,' Calla Lee said quickly. 'Why should it?'

'Indeed, why?' Karen supported. 'I always say being a good judge of character is more valuable than all the hearsay or newspaper talk in the West. But do tell me. How did you young folks get to meet?'

'It was just by chance,' the girl stated. 'Jesse was in Vista recovering from an accident. I was heading home and thought he would make an ideal escort.

So I offered him our hospitality in appreciation.'

'Vista . . . ?' Karen murmured and Ringo saw a strange look pass between the two women. Then her warm smile flashed again as she reached out to squeeze his hands. 'I'm sorry, I must have left my manners behind today. Do let our housekeeper show you to your room, Jesse. And we shall have that arm seen to when you are ready.'

'It's fine,' he replied, slinging saddle-bags over his shoulder. 'I doubt it will need any more fixing now. But I'd admire to wash up and take a look around. This has got to be about the finest spread I've seen.'

He vanished inside with the housekeeper leaving a sudden quiet in his wake.

*   *   *

It was a long time before either woman moved or spoke, and every vestige of animation drained from Karen Rainsford's face as she gestured imperiously to her daughter before leading the way along the gallery and towards the garden to enter the Spanish-style veranda alonside the main house.

When the woman whirled to face her daughter, Calla Lee held up an cautioning hand.

'Don't start carrying on until you know the facts, Mother.'

'Why did you bring this man here?'

This was not a mother's voice. It was the harsh accusing tone of one ruthless woman challenging another. For Karen and Calla Lee Rainsford were in reality about as far from the image of beautiful, wealthy and gracious ladyfolk of Monroe County as it was possible to imagine. In the privacy of this place and coming hard on the heels of Ringo's arrival, their transformation now was stark and dramatic.

'It was Mulvaney's suggestion,' snapped a taut-faced Calla Lee taking a brandy-bottle and glass from a cupboard and pouring herself two fingers. She drank half the liquor without blinking. She suddenly appeared far older and infinitely more world-weary than the fresh-faced girl Ringo had met in Vista. 'We suspected Ringo killed three of Mulvaney's riders out by the outlaw trail before they could stop off here. He seemed to think Jesse could be the Agency man Burke warned us about from Sweetgrass, and I guess I agree with him.'

Karen didn't blink an eye. She already knew of the killings on the outlaw trail. She might be fearful the law might be sniffing too close for comfort but none of this showed. She was shocked and angry and didn't believe in concealing her emotions.

'And so you allowed that conniving Mulvaney to persuade you to bring a possible Agency gun right here instead of dealing with him himself?'

The gloves were off, the cosy mother-daughter relationship of minutes ago replaced by something infinitely more one-sided and hard-edged.

'Mulvaney is waiting on Oakes to return from driving the last herd to

Montana. You know that. You can't blame him for not wanting to mess with a hired killer, if that is what Jesse is. And what better notion than to bring him here and make a fuss over him while we decide whether he's friend or enemy?'

'Jesse?'

'Pardon?'

'You just referred to him by his given name.'

'So?' Calla Lee's smile was wry as she raised the glass again. 'You may have noticed he's a very attractive man, Mother dearest.'

'You poor dumb little blonde! Attractive? You say that in one breath and in another admit he could be the most dangerous individual we have seen here since your father died.'

'Since you had him murdered, shouldn't you say?'

The sharp crack of Karen's hand against her daughter's cheek carried flat and hard across the garden. Calla Lee reeled, clutching her face. Karen appeared to be about to strike again when a side gate creaked open and wide-shouldered Joe Stranger approached the veranda. The gunman halted on sensing the tension. Suddenly Calla Lee rushed past her mother and ran into the house, leaving Karen breathing heavily, eyes dangerous.

'A criminal, philandering husband and a daughter without a brain in her head or respect for her own mother! And a partner, Mulvaney, who palms everything off on to me!' she fumed. 'Who says I have had it easy, Stranger? I dare anyone to say so. It's been hard for me all the way and . . . ' She cut herself off abruptly, fighting for control, getting it. She folded her arms and inhaled deeply. 'I don't have time for that kind of self-indulgence today. Well, what is it?'

Stranger jerked a thumb at the house. 'This geezer Miss Calla showed up with, ma'am. What's the story on him?'

'Why do you ask?'

'I just got a look at him and I don't like what I see. That there towhead is trouble, Miz Karen, it's stamped all over him. You hiring more gunpowder?'

'If I were it certainly would not be Mr Ringo. It's a long story but we suspect he could be law of some kind.'

'Law? Looks more like he walks the other side of the street, to me.' Stranger's face turned bleak as he stared inside the house. 'So how come you figure him thataway?'

Karen Rainsford compressed red lips. She had hired Stranger upon setting out on her campaign to convert Rolling Nine into the greatest cattle empire in the territory. The man was infatuated with her and was totally reliable, yet there was much she didn't confide in him. In truth, the more deeply involved in what for her were the dual careers of crime and ranching, the less she openly confided in anyone. She sensed it might prove lonely at the top, a price she would readily pay for getting there.

'Later, Joe. I've things to attend to. You and the men just keep handy. Any word from Oakes yet?'

'He said he expects to get back from Montana in a day or two.'

'He had better ... we just might need him ... '

'What? To deal with just one geezer?'

'When our own spy at Agency warned us that they might be sending a new man out here he was unable to give us a name or anything about this person at the time. But he says he believes he might be the most danger-ous man they have ever had on their books. If Jesse Ringo proves to be that man then we just might need all the manpower we can muster to deal with him.'

'But — '

'Enough for now,' Karen cut him off, snapping her fingers. 'Go!'

Sulking and sullen the hard man vanished leaving the woman pacing the veranda, divided skirt swishing about splendid legs, tigerish in her intensity as she reviewed unfolding events in her mind.

She realized she'd been hard on her

daughter today for reasons she didn't fully understand, but in retrospect found herself conceding that Calla Lee had certainly reacted smartly to the whiff of danger when she'd acted on Mulvaney's suggestion that she play up to the man then lure him back here where he could be assessed.

In many ways the mistress of Rolling Nine had enjoyed something of a dream run since she first sat down calmly one late night over a bottle of thirty-year-old Hermitage and conceived her sweeping plans to become the cattle queen of Wyoming.

That turning point in her life had come immediately and dramatically after her husband, who had shared one life as a stylish country gentleman here on Rolling Nine with herself and Calla Lee and another anonymous one as an outlaw and gun-smuggler, was shot dead.

Thus liberated, Karen considered her attributes and ambitions. She was an innately clever and ruthless person who suddenly had money, power, position and freedom. So she made her plans, set them in motion and had never looked back. The ranch prospered, her shady enterprises likewise. She grew strong and quickly became adept at delegating authority and establishing lines of command that would prove difficult to trace back to her should anything go amiss.

She had grown increasingly daring throughout the summer and well into fall before her high-priced mole in the governmental security system in Sweet-grass alerted that Agency were planning to drop in an undercover man to take the place of the murdered Bickner.

Because Burke insisted this action would be just one of the government's initiatives to tackle the Free Lands outlawry, and in light of the lack of any further information on this over the past week, Karen had been on the verge of downgrading his warning when news of the triple killing along the outlaw trail filtered through ahead of her daughter's return.

The three dead men had once worked with the Planer Oakes wild bunch in her then husband's gun-smuggling activities, which eventually became merely a cover diversion for the more lucrative rustling trade following her husband's death, when Oakes came to work for her.

The master plan to induce a state of lawlessness throughout the rangeland then capitalize on the chaos to reap a rich harvest from sweeping up the loose cattle had, regrettably, not been hers. But once she embraced a full partner-ship in the trade, following her husband's demise, she had doubled its size within six months through wider and better organization and tougher personnel.

Karen had shown herself to be a more than worthy replacement for her late husband in the crime stakes. She brooked no opposition be it from outlaws, gunmen or assorted scum who worked for the Karen dollar, her many lovers, business associates — even her own daughter.

Nor even from a mistrusted partner and opportunist like Indian Agent Mulvaney from Dark River!

Her eyes glittered.

She hated to admit her indebtedness to Mulvaney. While Buck had initially so impressed her with the manner in which he'd opened up this part of Wyoming to his gun-running operation, it had been Mulvaney who'd first recognized the true potential of the fallout from that crime wave.

Suddenly, while gun-runners' Winchesters turned the plains smoke-grey and blood-red, the ranchers began to flee their spreads with the result that thousands of homeless cattle were left to wander the Free Lands. Mulvaney, a man with a secret owlhoot background, had recognized his opportunity and promptly rounded up a herd which he'd run up to a crooked beef-packer in Montana, notching up huge profits.

Karen had been impressed when

Stranger accidentally stumbled on to Mulvaney's infant operation. The biggest step she'd ever taken was to approach Mulvaney and propose a partnership, otherwise she'd shop him to the law. The man accepted and she launched into her new career with skill and gusto some time before she decided to break free of old ties. She secretly informed on her then husband, Buck, to the government, resulting in his execution at the hands of an Agency hit man. In full charge of Rolling Nine thereafter, Karen quickly gained the strong hand in her early relationship with Mulvaney and had been exerting it ever since.

The Indian Agent was a mean s.o.b. who just might bring her down if their relationship continued to deteriorate. But Karen knew how to hold on to a man by exploiting his weaknesses. The greedy Indian Agent's other weakness was young women, and Karen had simply and cold-bloodedly given him her daughter, just to keep him contented while she waited for the right opportunity to prepare his death.

But overnight a new danger had reared its head and it had a new name. Jesse Ringo.

By an act of will she had regained composure by the time she leaned her elbows on the wooden balcony and gazed across her lovely gardens; soon she was thinking clearly again.

'If Ringo is the Agency man then he has probably already alerted headquarters he was on his way here,' she breathed aloud. Then hard on the heels of this disturbing thought came another. Hadn't she caught Ringo studying her too intently upon their meeting? She'd imagined he'd been taking in every detail of her appearance with special attention to her hair . . . whatever in God's name that might imply . . .

'Rubbish, mother!' Calla Lee retorted when Karen confided her concerns some time later. 'You shouldn't fret so. Ringo couldn't possibly have any reason to suspect we'd be involved in anything. You've been far too careful covering our tracks. It's just his job to check out places like ours. We shall have to just stay cool, play the ladies and eventually he'll be off looking for real outlaws, not refined ladies of quality and character.'

The girl's manner was mocking, bitter. But underneath she was terrified of her mother, with good reason. She believed Karen had had her father murdered. Haines had been a criminal and worse, but he was her father.

'But what if you're wrong? What if he has already uncovered us and Agency is at this very moment alerting the law and the marshals and perhaps even the Army to come investigate? They could be closing in right at this moment and — '

'Oh, do hush, Mother. You're acting like a hysterical housewife, fearful the parson might have heard she likes a tipple. Do pull yourself together.'

Her pride affronted, Karen did as ordered. In moments she was again coldly poised and back in control, her mind leaping ahead.

'Of course we're obviously making this more complicated and threatening than it need be.' She spread her hands. 'After all, if we are under any kind of threat it's all encapsulated in one man at this stage . . . '

'What do you mean? What are you thinking? I know that look.'

Karen smiled coldly.

'Never you mind — honey. Can you persuade Ringo to drive into town with you? Get him to visit Doc Jordan to look at his arm, perhaps? Any excuse.'

'Perhaps,' said Calla Lee. 'But why?'

'Leave that to me. Now please go tell Stranger and Ward I wish to see them immediately.'

'Whatever you say, Mother dear.'

'And, Calla Lee . . . '

The girl paused. 'Yes?'

'You might as well know I've been far from happy with you lately. You've been too withdrawn, too fond of your own company, secretive. A person in my

172

position could become very paranoid about that sort of behaviour and might be tempted to react against it. Do you understand what I'm saying?'

'Why, Mother, it almost sounds as if you are threatening me!'

'Yes, it rather does, doesn't it.'

'I won't tolerate that — I refuse to accept that sort of thing any longer.'

'You'll accept what I dish out, young lady. Just remember, when it came time for us to rid ourselves of your father and his pernicious, amoral ways, it was all left to me to arrange. You just stood back and wept like a cissy even though you knew he had to go. And I've built the empire. It was I who incorporated Mulvaney, organized our partnership, all the details, even though I had to almost force you at gunpoint to play your part with that thieving scum. You've been nothing but a drag and an irritation, but you should realize that if I was capable of ridding myself of dead weight once I can do so again.'

The sheer force of the attack

shattered Calla Lee's brittle defiance. Bursting into sudden tears the girl ran for the door. Her mother was quicker. Karen seized her by the hand and slapped her face. Hard. Calla Lee gasped in shock and pain, was struck again.

'You think you're so pretty!' Karen accused. 'Think every man is mad about you. Well, you are wrong about that too, you dismal little nobody. I'm the one.' She slapped her again. 'Say it, you bitch of a girl. Mother is the one!'

The ugly sounds echoed through the house to be overheard by the maids, the Filipino houseboy, the housekeeper, the cook — and by the Rolling Nine's solitary house-guest.

Ringo appeared from the kitchen where he'd been quietly questioning the staff. He reached the entryway to the huge parlour and came to an abrupt halt.

Calla Lee had half-fallen against a sofa, her hands protectively up to her face. Karen was still swinging at her and swearing like a muleskinner.

The woman gasped as steel fingers closed over her right wrist. She whirled to glare wildly into Ringo's face, her sudden irrational rage stripping her face of all glamour and beauty to reveal the ugliness beneath.

'How dare you . . . you bum!' she shrieked, fighting him. 'Who invited you here? Not me. Well, you're not fooling me for a minute. I know who you — ' She broke off, realizing temper was taking her too far. But she was still angry enough to rake him with her nails. Ringo shoved her away and she tumbled to the floor just as a side door opened and trouble in tandem came striding into the room.

'What the tarnation . . . ?' snarled big Stranger, dropping hand to gunbutt. 'Get away from the boss lady, saddle bum. Now!'

'Sure I will,' Ringo replied. He took Calla Lee by the hand and raised the sobbing girl from the couch as Karen lunged to her feet, wild-eyed and dishevelled. 'But keep your paws clear of your shooters, both of you. That sort of thing makes me nervous.'

Stranger and Ward looked from him to Karen, waiting for orders.

'She attacked me,' Karen panted. 'The dumb little sugar-pop had the gall. Then Goldilocks intervened. He . . . he hurt me, boys.'

That was their cue. The pair came in like the pros they were. Instantly Ringo released his grip on the girl and balanced himself on the balls of his feet to throw a punch in runty Ward's direction. It was just a feint. In the same motion he pivoted from the hips to catch a lunging Stranger with a pistoning blow to the mouth which snapped teeth and drew crimson.

Stranger was hitting the floor like a sack of wheat when Calla Lee shrieked a warning:

'Jesse, watch out!'

Ringo whipped a sixshooter from leather even as he whirled. Eli Ward was fast and his mean little face was

176

suffused with fury as his blue-barrelled .44 came snaking up from the hip, finger curled round the trigger, all five feet five of him radiating lethal intent.

Ringo was faster.

He fired and Ward went skittering backwards, spurs hooking in the rug to bring him crashing down with the .44 spinning from his grasp, blood pumping from his gun arm.

'Try to hurt me, sunshine, I'll hurt you,' Ringo hissed.

He swung to cover Stranger who was up but sick as a rabid polecat. Stranger wanted to draw, thought seriously about it for about one second, but couldn't do it. Ringo had him cold and the Nine's top gun knew it.

Karen Rainsford appeared speechless with emotion and seemed to feel it necessary to put a leather sofa between her and the man with the gun. The doorway was now crowded with ashen-faced servants. Outside, men were shouting and boots thudded on the porches. There appeared to be just one cool head at Rolling Nine headquarters at that pregnant moment. Ringo. He took a white-faced Calla Lee by the arm and led her towards the hallway, motioning the servants aside with his pistol.

'I don't know what the hell this is all about,' he warned the room, 'although maybe I will in time. Right now, I'm going, but I'm not leaving anybody behind for you to beat up on, lady. If you're smart you'll order your people not to try and stop us. If they do anything foolish, don't make any plans for the rest of the week. You'll be too busy attending funerals.'

This was gunfighter tough talk which he rarely employed. But sometimes it worked, and this proved such a time. Seemingly dazed by violence which she herself did not control, Karen obligingly croaked the orders and twenty people stood back and watched the gunfighter and the girl ride out minutes later to make for the Hudville trail.

'She's done it again,' Karen muttered

as she splashed brandy into a huge snifter glass. 'Betrayed me. You'd think even a little ninny like her would have learned from her father's . . . misfortune.'

Once again the mistress of Rolling Nine had to curb her tongue. It was that sort of a day. Alone in the parlour later, she realized the first double brandy didn't help much, so she took another. She still felt more at risk than at any time since taking her destiny into her own hands and reaching for the stars. It took the arrival of a band of armed riders, coming in across the open rangeland, to lift her spirits.

The return of Planer Oakes and his wild bunch could scarcely have been better timed.

8

HAVOC AT HUDVILLE

The cryptic message simply read: *assistance on the way.*

No signature. But Ringo knew its origin. He'd nominated Hudville to Agency as his contact point when sending his last wire from Vista. He could only guess at what form this assistance might take, where it originated, or how long it might be coming his way.

He found Calla Lee composed by the time he returned to the Globe Hotel. The way she jumped up from the lobby chair at his arrival caused a pleasant, slow-fading tightness in his chest. He didn't really know her and knew he should not trust her, yet such factors seemed as irrelevant as spindrift somehow. Something strange and exhilarating was working in him. Men who learn to fight before they can walk, to kill before they ride and make a religion of independence and self-sufficiency, think differently from other men.

He'd been solid ready to kill people sooner than see her harmed out at the spread, he knew. That sort of thing gave a man something to think about. He was conscious of a curious nonchalance in his attitude as she accompanied him to have his arm strapped up again, then took her to a back street bar for coffee. He'd stirred up a hornets' nest at Rolling Nine and he had a strong sense of events rolling towards some kind of resolution here in Hudville. Yet he was still relaxed, like a man who might want to believe the storms might pass them by in this placid little backwater, tucked away from the storms of reality.

Her eyes were on him as he returned from the bar with the pannikins of coffee. 'You really are very sweet,' she said as he sat.

'It might come as a surprise but

nobody's ever called me that before.'
He looked into blue eyes and heard
himself say quietly: 'I am law you know.
No, not the regular kind. I'm as
irregular as can be. I'm a gunman they
hijacked into playing detective for them
. . . they wanted somebody who could
play the game and not get shot.' He
tapped his bandaged arm. 'Turned out
I wasn't quite that good.'

'I'm sure now that I knew what you
were the moment I set eyes on you. I
was afraid at first, knowing the threat
you posed for just about everyone I
know. I told Mulvaney what I thought,
then agreed to bring you out knowing
you could be killed. But somehow I
stopped being afraid of you, isn't that
strange?'

'Well, I hate to tell you but by any
fool yardstick you like to use I'm
someone to be afraid of, Calla Lee. But
who are you? I mean, really?'

The questions had to be asked now,
veils stripped away. He had witnessed
enough at the spread to be intensely

suspicious of everyone on it. But he needed information in order to figure his next move, and as it could only come from her, he knew he'd play it hard if he must.

He soon realized this wasn't necessary. Somewhere between quitting Vista in his company and sitting here in this almost empty bar with a fire burning in the hearth, Calla Lee had decided she had had enough.

Quietly, almost gratefully, she related her story beginning with her father's criminality, his death at the hands of Agency, her mother's filling her father's outlaw shoes; Karen's alliance with Mulvaney, her offering her own daughter to the Indian Agent to appease his wounded vanity when she gained superiority over him, as she did over everyone. Or had done.

Enough of the life that had been forced upon her, that was. She may have made this momentous decision to speak out before, had she had someone to turn to. She now believed she had found that someone, and while she had the opportunity, talk she would. He had been frank with her, she would be the same with him.

★   ★   ★

The little fire popped and the day was wearing on. It was not a pretty story which Jesse Ringo heard through and he didn't expect it to be.

Ringo signalled to the bar for more drinks. Coffee again. He was still strangely relaxed but did not expect it to last. From what Calla Lee had revealed concerning Karen, Mulvaney and their respective gangs of criminals backed by what he'd witnessed at the ranch, and his wire from Agency, a clear head in Hudville today might mean the difference between living to see another sunrise or not. You could smell the danger, yet Ringo had rarely felt less attracted by it. Crazily, he wanted time simply to unfold by week and by month with his Colts remaining in their holsters where they belonged, with Calla Lee and her big blue eyes always close, and everyone else acting like brothers.

This was pure fantasy from a man who rarely dreamed, who lived adventure and challenge, the more dangerous the better.

It was unreal and yet strangely powerful, like a child wishing a dream to come true.

But this was surely no way for a two-gun troubleshooter to operate. And soon the fantasy faded and he was Ringo again, the Agency gunman with a job to finish if he didn't want to shake hands with the hangman again. Life didn't get much more real than this.

'What's that racket, you figure?'

A drinker's query to the barkeep reached their ears just as Ringo became aware of the rumble of hoofbeats. Instantly alert the couple rose to go to the window. The girl clutched at his arm when a squad of horsemen hove into sight with Jed Mulvaney at their head.

'Oh, Jesse. He was waiting for Oakes — that's that man in black — to contact him in Vista, at the time when you ran foul of Oakes's three gunmen. Mulvaney doesn't give a toss about losing men, but Planer Oakes does. They must have come up here to make sure Karen had you killed as a suspected Agency man. I know it.'

He stared at her as fog drifted by the windows.

'Then Mulvaney really expected Karen to finish me off? Where would he get that notion?'

'I told him . . . so he wouldn't come after you with the men . . . '

He almost smiled at that.

'It could have worked . . . '

'Jesse, I had to warn Jed that mother was planning to destroy him. I just couldn't see any more people die for her insane ambition.'

'Maybe nobody will.'

She gazed up at him. 'You don't really believe that, do you?'

'No.'

* ★ ★

Somehow lamp-lighting time had come and gone without one shot having been heard on the quiet streets of Hudville.

Ringo gazed up at the winter sky and judged it to be around eight. Leaning against the corral fence beside the livery barn in a knifing wind, he had been maintaining a close watch on the streets ever since dropping Calla Lee off at friends on Wolf Street.

Paradoxically, for a smallish town playing host to a dozen dangerous men with guns tonight, Hudville was very quiet. But it wasn't an easy kind of quiet. The opposite. The town seemed to be holding its breath, waiting for something to happen. He could feel the tension crackling like electricity in the air, heralding a tornado. Hostility, fear, doubt, suspicion — all the uncertain elements that could lead to violence but not quite violent yet.

Citizens who'd never seen dangerous men in force before were expecting

187

trouble any moment. Yet they just couldn't stay away from the smell of trouble. Mobs of citizens were congregated at the Black Spur and Easyrider, still drinking, talking and waiting for something.

The search for Ringo continued. They knew he was here now and were sworn to get him. The word had gone out that he'd uncovered the guilt of Rolling Nine and Dark River Agency and had to die before what he knew spread like a flood tide across the Wyoming Territory.

★   ★   ★

Mulvaney had brought Planer Oakes with him to Hudville from Vista to help ensure Ringo didn't see another dawn, and *en route* had met up with the Rolling Nine's gun crew. It was Karen Rainsford who'd alerted her men that Ringo was an Agency man and couldn't be let live.

Long after dark both Mulvaney and

Joe Stranger had most of their men still out on the streets searching for their man while the women and children of Hudville cowered behind locked doors and the most wanted man in town smoked easily on his pipe and moved through the light and shadow like a wraith, watching, listening and elusive as a cougar on the prowl.

No sign of the town's single peace officer on these streets. Nor the mayor, the painted women or the local holy man railing against sin. Nobody but men bristling with guns searching alleys, barns and doorways for a yellow-haired man with two Colts and a reputation that seemed to be growing bloodier in imagination the longer the search continued.

If there was any way this night could slip by without some fool getting his head blown off, Ringo couldn't see it.

But he would not run; and odds were just mathematics anyway. Or so he assured himself as a pair of swaggering searchers toting lighted torches drew closer, forcing him back against a barn's high wall.

He reflected that most of his life had been spent in combat of one kind or another. Combat against childhood neglect, bad Indians and worse white men. Against the odds and always against those things he hated such as cruelty, crime, corruption and the misuse of power — like Agency.

He was ready to fight here in Hudville but only if there was no other way.

He now found himself moving even further back into the shadows, inching away from trouble as he'd never done before. And knew the reason why.

To qualify as a real gunslinger, a man's first and most vital attribute had to be not giving a damn if he lived or died, he told himself. From this rare source many a great gunslinger had sprung. He might well have been born with that quality, or had certainly acquired it along the way.

But tonight this was no longer the case.

He cared.

She had made him care.

Impossible!

He cleared his mind and suddenly realized that a bow-legged ranny with jug ears and a sawed-off in his hands had sat to rest upon the stone watertrough by the laneway in full lamplight not thirty feet distant. The man was speaking to a party Ringo could not see.

'If you ask me the hotshot's fifty miles away by now and pickin' up speed. I say let's forget him and go git us some of the Planers. Bastards have been lording it over us Dark River boys ever since they got back from Montana, and I reckon even the boss would expect us to crimp their style for 'em if we got a chance.'

'You talk too much, Hoagy,' came a disembodied voice. 'Us and Rollin' Nine's too even-matched for startin' in on one another . . . '

The voices were snatched away by a gust of wind. The unseen Ringo took the dead pipe from his lips, and ran a

191

patch through the barrel of his right-hand .45.

Trouble in the ranks, he reflected. But he couldn't rely on that coming to much, he supposed.

He kept thinking of the girl, how like him she was underneath. She had a family and it stank. He had folks someplace but they weren't up to much, so that stank too. He and she were the loners, except when together.

A shadowy figure came from behind shrubs off to his left, and Ringo felt his neck hair rise. The man was very bulky but moved easily in a low crouch. There was a big black gun in his fist and he was focused on the man by the water-trough. If this crackerhead was mistaking him for himself, then he needed his eyesight tended to.

He felt his eyes snap wide as the stealthy figure dropped to one knee, rested the barrel of his Colt on his upraised left forearm and laid a bead on the unsuspecting shotgunner thirty yards away.

The roar of the shot slammed across the streets, shivered the trees and rattled the rooftops as the Mulvaney rider tumbled slowly backwards into the trough and sank from sight.

Before the first echo had died away, the assassin whirled and started back past the corral to pass briefly through a patch of lamplight. The crooked nose, the catfish mouth, the bulging jaw and lumpy forehead: Ringo instantly recognized that figure from his recent past.

Herman.

They'd met briefly and violently the day he arrived at Agency from the Three Rivers Death House when the heavyweight tried to muscle him around and had his ugly face smashed in for his pains.

Herman equalled Agency!

What the hell was he doing here? And why had he gunned a man down that way when this whole town was on edge?

Powerful legs carried the shooter round the dark end of the livery barn as

Hudville exploded into uproar. The powerful figure running along the barn wall was travelling at full pace when Ringo sprang from the shadows swinging his cutter like a club.

The barrel dropped the heavyweight in his tracks.

Seizing a handful of shirt-front, Ringo lugged the moaning figure to the barn's side door and dragged him inside. A slug rang off a pump handle outside and ricocheted up into the stars. It was Rolling Nine against Mulvaney out there, thanks to one bullet in the back. The lid was blowing off Hudville and the man responsible lay half choking in Ringo's fierce grip as he slapped his bloody face one way, then the other.

'Why did you do that, you mad bastard?' he raged. 'Why?'

'J-Judas — Ringo, where'd you spring from — '

The man's words were chopped off as a backhander almost caused his head to spin off his neck.

'Why?' Ringo repeated. 'And who are you with, you fat shoat?'

'C-Carmody of course. And the Chief is in Vista — along with a couple of the men. We were heading for the ranch when we learned you were in trouble with bunches heading your way — and not all that far away. So Carmody told us to get here pronto. Real glad you're still alive, Ringo.'

He held up both hands as Ringo got ready to sock him again.

'Why are Carmody and Westerman to hell and gone out here, you bastard?'

'Hell, I thought you'd figure. To help you wash it all up. And when they learned you were likely in town with all these outlaws looking to do you in, he figured things real fast . . . you know, the way Mr Carmody does. He sent me into town to stage a diversion, man. Told me to spook these bastards and maybe get the towners tying into them and — '

'A diversion? You said a diversion. From what?'

'Why, I reckoned you'd have figured. From the main job, of course.' Herman panted as Ringo allowed him to sit up. He looked like hell but he could talk straight now. 'The Rainsford dame, or should I say . . . Haines?'

'Haines?' Ringo stepped back back from the man. Gunshots were sounding a block away. There was no guessing what hell was breaking loose as a hard-ridden horse hurtled by. 'How did you know . . . ?'

'Headquarters done it. After you tipped them about these Rainsfords they turned Records ass up and discovered Helmut Haines had changed his name legal to Rainsford before buying up the Rolling Nine. When they wired your sheriff here, and he told the Chief how rich Rainsford had got before we nailed him, and how his missus had doubled the family fortune over the last six months, it didn't take long to figure she had to be carrying on in the lawbreaking business — rustling was our best guess. So that's why we showed so damn fast.'

'What's Carmody doing while you're here?' Ringo feared he might already know the answer to that.

'Doing? He's took off to settle things permanent, of course. Crush the head of the snake, he called it. That's the brief they gave you, remember? But you've been moving too slow and we've been on borrowed time down at Agency for weeks. Nail the outlaws or get ready to shut up shop — that's what the government told the Chief. So your uncovering Rolling Nine just came in the nick of time, Ringo, and Mr Carmody says we owe 'most all of it to you. Say, why you looking so peculiar, man?'

'Shut up!' Ringo snarled. 'Are you saying Carmody's planning to kill Karen Rainsford? Not arrest her?'

Herman did his best to smirk with his ruined mouth.

'Mister, you're new to Agency but you ought to know how we work. You want someone arrested, you go see the marshals. But if you want something wrapped up, filed away and finished for keeps, Agency is your stop-off place. Yessir, you can wager Haines's widow won't be running Winchesters into Indian Lands or flooding Montana with stolen beef after tonight. No siree, Bob!'

Ringo rose stiffly to his feet. Sure, he'd suspected Agency's methods, but hadn't anticipated they might respond so swiftly, especially against a woman. He felt ice in his veins as he watched Herman haul his damaged bulk erect and somehow to stay standing.

'I can't believe Carmody would risk committing murder.'

'Hell, not him personal. Not the second in command himself. Didn't I say he's got company? Barlowe and Tucker. Tucker was honing those big knives of his when I left them out by the windmill.'

Tucker!

Shock drained all colour from Ringo's face as he backed away. He envisioned Karen Rainsford's feminine body coming up against the rending steel of that butcher's knives. He twisted his head at a fresh crash of sound. Brawling figures were visible on Doolin Street now. Everybody in town was geared up for trouble, and liquor and excitement were proving irresistible combustibles. Likely those out-of-towners had already forgotten what the hell had brought them here by this.

Not that he gave one plug damn about them. Suddenly he knew what he had to do. But first there was Herman.

The ape man didn't even see the blow coming. The Colt barrel smashed the side of his skull and he dropped like a shot dog. Ringo stepped over the big body and took a back lane for Wolf Street.

The last place Calla Lee should be tonight was out at the ranch. But there wasn't another place he dared leave her. Not with Westerman, Carmody and other Agency killers on the loose, there wasn't.

It was only two blocks to Jilly Black's

cottage on Wolf. Blowing hard, he identified himself at the back door and the girl's scared face quickly appeared at the window.

'Tell Calla Lee to come quick, Jilly,' he said urgently. 'I've got to get her out of here — '

'Jesse, she's gone.'

'What?'

'You were so long she got scared. When she realized her mother was out at the spread with just the servants and one or two men, she grew fearful for her safety, what with all the fighting and all, and — Jesse, where are you going?'

He was already gone.

9

HARD WAY TO DIE

Karen's tone was scornful.

'You had to come out and look after your mother! You must think I was born yesterday if I'd believe that. You came running home for the same reason you always do. Because the big, bad world is just too much for innocent little Calla Lee, and you need momma to protect you. What's new, honey? God knows where you got your cissy ways from. It wasn't from your father and they certainly didn't come from me. But seeing as you're here you might as well make yourself useful. Pour me a whiskey. Straight.'

'Mother,' Calla Lee pleaded. 'You have no idea what's happening down in Hudville — '

'Of course I do. Our boys and

Mulvaney's are flushing out your dirty boyfriend, and by now he should be swinging from Hudville's peppercorn tree if there's any justice. Then they'll probably brawl the way they generally do when they come together, but that's just because they don't have any brains and can't quite forget when they used to be on opposite sides. All that matters is that Ringo will be gone, and when the dust settles we'll still have both the guns and the cows and . . . where is that whiskey?'

There were tears in Calla Lee's eyes as she moved to the sideboard. The great house was unnaturally quiet, and she could hear the roaring of the flooded stream in back of the barn. She'd encountered just two men standing watch outside, while the servants were huddled in back somewhere, terrified and wondering how many of their husbands and boyfriends would return from Hudville. She carried the drink to Karen and watched her taste it as if she were a stranger. All her life this girl had fought to come to terms with the fact that both her parents were strange and dangerous creatures quite unlike other people she knew, other girls' folks. They plundered, robbed and killed for money, and she had always strongly suspected that Karen had informed on her father to the law, resulting in his death and thus enabling Karen to seize the reins. She knew for a fact that Karen had paid Osage Smith to kill Agency's new field man on learning of his appointment.

Karen had even forced her into an affair with Jed Mulvaney in order to cement their alliance in the rustling operation. She had obeyed as she always had done; she knew no other course.

But things were different now. She had a wonderful secret to tell her mother about herself and Jesse Ringo. If she could just get her to listen, make Karen realize that her life had changed and that she could not continue this crazy life on the ranch now she had at last fallen in love, then maybe her mother might begin thinking and acting like a real mother. Call the men off in Hudville, accept Jesse, give up the rustling and settle down to a decent respectable life while there was still time. She wanted her to quit the headquarters with her right now, until the bloody chaos was resolved. Return to sanity before it was all too late.

'Mother, Mother darling — '

'What was that?' Karen cut her off, turning to the windows.

'What was what?'

'I thought I heard something in the yard. Make yourself useful. Do go and take a look.'

Obediently Calla Lee quit the huge room to make her way down the silent hallway to the front gallery. The ranch yard stood wide and empty under the starlight, the creek roaring and sparkling with ice beyond the east wing as always at this time of year. There was no other sound, nothing unusual. But as the girl turned to go back inside, she paused and took a second look, her hand flying to her throat.

There was no longer a sentry by the ranch yard gate!

*   *   *

At first Ringo thought it was a dead animal sprawled in shadows by the bunkhouse wall but, as he eased closer, a gun in each hand, he saw, with a sudden tightening of his throat, that it was the body of a man.

Instantly his eyes flicked across the yard, the outbuildings, the lights of the house. On riding in from the trail he had sensed something unnatural about the atmosphere enveloping Rolling Nine headquarters that set his neck hair lifting, prompting him to ditch the horse and come in afoot.

It took but one corpse to confirm that his fears and instincts were operating only too well.

But had he gotten here too late?

He stepped closer to stare down at

the small body, the wide, staring eyes and the gaping purple lips of the jagged knife wound that had cut the throat to the bone.

And thought: Tucker!

His heart clenched in his chest for an agonized moment as his gaze cut this way and that. This was nothing like his customary disciplined reaction to violent death — and he knew why. The cause of the sudden shaking, sweating and shuddering with convulsive breath wasn't fear for himself, but for her! Where was Calla Lee? Where were Tucker, Carmody, Barlowe, Karen? And surely the headquarters had more than just one nighthawk tonight!

He darted towards the gates before forcing himself to a stop. With the tumbling creek cutting along one side of the house and the light of post lamps flooding the raked gravel expanse of the yard, there was no way he could make it across to the main house unseen if anyone was watching, and he had to believe there would be.

The house stood before him, silent as the grave.

Only one thing for it.

'Carmody!'

His shout echoed hollowly. No response. But had he seen a curtain flicker?

'Carmody, you bast — ' He cut himself off, fingering his sixgun handles. Don't antagonize them, Jesse. Don't let your fear for her addle your brain. She could well be all right. She had to be. Surely they wouldn't . . . ?

'Carmody . . . er, Mr Carmody. If you're there, let's talk and — ' He broke off as emotion got the better of him, fear gripping his vitals as he roared at the top of his lungs. 'Calla Lee! If you're OK, let me know!'

A sound came from the house, then the voice.

'You don't sound friendly, Agent Ringo. Why are you so angry? Of course I'm here. We all are. Better disarm if you want to parley, otherwise we might have to treat you like a hostile.'

'How the hell did you get here so fast?' Ringo retorted, eyes cutting in every direction. 'And why? Or can I guess?'

No response. The creek gurgled and splashed. He was cold all over as he sensed hidden guns lining up on him from shadowed rooms.

Jesse Ringo took the gamble of his life.

It was one of the hardest things he'd ever had to do, to turn his back now and go strolling off between bunkhouse and barn, every second half-expecting either a bullet or a cowhide-hafted big blade to thud between his shoulder blades.

It didn't happen.

They either didn't want to kill him, or still hoped to con him into coming in, where they could make dead sure of getting him.

But the gamble paid off and suddenly he was in deep shadows, sweating a freshet and eyes stabbing in every direction. His heart was a hammer. He desperately wanted to charge the house down in Injun style, guns bucking and screaming a Sioux war cry to confuse the enemy. But he couldn't risk getting chopped to pieces there in that star-sheened yard and maybe leaving the girl he loved in a house with an animal that walked upright like a man.

He was going by the tackroom moments later when a horse whickered sharply close by. Ringo hit dirt and rolled a split second before Carmody's shout jarred the silence.

'Barlowe! He's yours!'

He dropped flat as he caught a swift blur of movement in ornamental shrubs by the horse yard. He rolled again as gunflame blossomed and he both heard and felt the slug whistle overhead. Then he opened up and tracers of death leapt across open space to be swallowed by shadows and shrubs. Ringo sprang erect and jumped left, then right, working his triggers again when a single shot flared at him, the bark of the hidden gun followed by a strangled gasp of total agony.

He held his fire as a heavy shape rose drunkenly from the shrubbery and staggered into the open, hands clutching his chest, vomiting blood. He crashed down and did not move again. His right arm was outflung, his smoking Colt still in his hand.

Ringo reloaded with feverish haste. Now he knew why they hadn't opened up from the house. Barlowe had been in close and should have got him. But he hadn't. Instead it was he who was lying dead. But what did this say about Calla Lee? Was she still alive? Was anybody alive but the killers?

Pausing only to reload he darted back along the bunkhouse wall then vaulted the white-painted houseyard railing fence to land lightly and sprint a zigzag course.

Instantly a rifle churned from the direction of the tank stand, but the shot was wild. He poured on the coal to veer right suddenly and dash headlong across the very centre of the yard with the house looming before him.

Now was the time to shoot and holler and pray Tucker's nerves might prove vulnerable under pressure. Carmody — it had to be him — kept shooting wildly from the tank stand as Ringo's stretching legs reached for the steps just as the front-room light blinked out, plunging the front of the house into darkness.

He was lunging desperately across the darkened gallery when a searing pain caught him high in the chest, then his forehead. He was falling and clutching his chest when his head smashed into the door-frame and the world turned black.

★ ★ ★

Calla Lee fought back panic as she fumbled in the bureau for the gun. She was in her mother's office, knew she kept a weapon here somewhere.

A scream.

The girl whirled at the sound, biting

her tongue to avoid giving her position away to whoever or whatever it was that was in the house with her.

They'd been watching for sign of the missing sentries from the parlour a brief time earlier when a strange sound from the hallway alerted them to closer danger. With typical courage Karen had gone striding out, only to draw up with a cry on sighting the body of the Filipino houseboy sprawled against the staircase steps in a spreading pool of blood.

That was where the nightmare began — when the women slammed and locked the parlour door then quit the room together through the window that gave on to the glass-enclosed side gallery on the east side overlooking the creek.

There was a killer in the house and he was coming after them.

Somehow they became separated by the servants' quarters, as one by one the house lights were snuffed out by someone they had not yet even seen,

Karen apparently heading for her gun room leaving Calla Lee in darkness and fear — as she had done many times in their unhappy lives together.

The girl's hand closed over the cold steel of the .38 as gunfire broke out from the direction of the bunkhouses. Calla Lee did not know whether to scream for help and run the risk of giving away her position to the intruder, or take her courage in her hand and go after him.

She chose the latter course, darting light-footed down the side passageway towards the gun room — while rifles and pistols continued to snarl and bellow outside.

She lurched to a halt as the front room's big light went out and someone laughed.

'Mother!' she cried. She couldn't help it. A moment later she sensed more than saw the figure framed in the front-room doorway.

Calla Lee froze. The intruder had his back to her. In silhouette against the light he was a shambling hairy ape of a man with heavy shoulders and something dripping from his right hand on to the polished floorboards.

Her hand flew to her mouth. It was blood.

'End of the road, Miz Karen,' a rasping voice whispered. Then the shambling figure moved aside and Calla Lee saw the familiar figure sprawled on her back by the settee, the haft of a throwing-knife protruding from her breast.

Her mother was dead. She knew it instantly. She began to sob. The figure whirled, leather sheaths flapping against its hips. She caught the glint of feral joy in shadowed eyes as they lighted upon her.

Next moment Tucker went reeling backwards as she raised her pistol with astonishing calm and fired, the sound of the weapon in the confined space booming like a cannon.

Enraged, the Agency killer clawed at the bullet agony in his right flank with his left hand, then for the handle of the huge belt-knife with his right. Teeth clenched and seemingly more animal than man in his fury, he dived into the hallway as the girl whirled and ran.

He knew she would have to look back. And she did. Tucker somersaulted across the intervening space, bringing both boots up together to strike her gun hand as she cut loose at his blurring shape.

The gun tumbled free and Tucker was on his feet, a hideous figure with that dirty fringe hanging over his eyes, blood soaking his pants, twisted sideways with the pain, yet grinning like a ghoul from hell.

'Bitch, you are gonna die . . . and it's gonna be good.'

Light shimmered on the blade of the huge knife as he lunged and swung his weapon with all his strength.

The blow missed and the girl spun and ran like a startled deer.

★ ★ ★

He was in hell and all the demons were shrieking.

That was Ringo's first thought as the fog of unconsciousness began to lighten. With blood from his gashed chest running freely and throbbing agony in his temples, he grew aware that he was lying cramped up against a wall by a door with his brain spinning like a ferris wheel, clawing for reality but unable to get a grasp on it.

Then he remembered what had lifted him from unconsciousness, and knew now that it had been a human voice screaming. A woman's voice!

'Calla Lee!'

Full awareness returned with an agonizing jolt and he was rolling up on to hands and knees staring stupidly at something lying on the boards beneath him.

A knife. He thought he'd been shot, now he realized he'd ducked at the vital moment as someone in the darkness had hurled the big blade, which instead of killing him had ripped his chest, flipped over, and the big steel haft had smashed into his forehead, knocking him cold.

Without hesitation he grabbed the handle and hefted the weapon. It stank. It was one of Tucker's blades.

Tucker!

With a gun in one hand and a knife in the other he charged recklessly through the doorway, skidded on blood-soaked boards.

The house was silent.

Easing his way to the opened front-room window, Ringo slid a leg over the sill, ducked beneath the raised window and was inside.

A door opening on to a hallway stood ajar and there was a light out there somewhere. He was halfway across the room when he heard the whisper of leather against wood. Ringo froze, senses quivering. His nostrils flared. That smell. Body stink. Tucker. Tucker was close.

Cheyenne tutors had taught him to move without any sound at all before he had had enough baby teeth to chew buffalo meat.

He made it to the door in time to see a familiar hunched figure disappear round a corner leading to the creek side of the house.

He didn't go after his man, his eyes cutting to the sprawled figure on the floor. Heedless of anything else now, he rushed to Karen's side, groaning inwardly when he saw what the knife had done.

He closed the staring eyes and rose slowly, eyes glittering like an animal's. The silent steps of the hunting wolf took him to the east-wing corner where blood splotches led off towards the drawing-room doorway.

He followed them, slowing at the sound of heavy breathing discernible above the murmur of the stream outside. He put an eye to the chink between door and doorframe. Tucker was slumped in a chair at a rosewood table with a brandy bottle in his hand, a red-stained pants' leg and a dreamy

218

smile on his grotesque face.

Portrait of a butcher. And what had Carmody said? That Ringo hated Tucker because they were so alike. He shook his head; that couldn't be right. How could they be alike when he was alive and this man was dead.

The bottle thudded to the floor from Tucker's hand as this glitter-eyed, blood-spattered apparition ghosted into the room to loom before him like the prophet of doom come down from the mountain.

'No!' he croaked, heaving out of his chair. 'I killed you out front. I never miss.'

'You didn't miss the woman.' Ringo's voice was strange, trigger fingers itching on cocked Colts as he watched the killer's right hand, flat and hairy like some animal, stealing towards the handle of the huge knife in the belt scabbard. Ringo housed his Colts. An incredulous look flashed across Tucker's face and the lightning-fast hand pounced on to the knife.

Ringo let fly with a karate kick that crashed into the hand and damn near broke it. He lunged, ripping the sheath from the belt and thrusting it through his own, his expression slightly manic in the light as he stepped back.

'Take it,' he said. 'You like cutting people, and you are good at it. All you must do is take the knife and kill me with it. More chance than you gave them, don't you know?'

Tucker was standing. The man might be as ugly as a whore's dream, and was packing lead, but he still radiated brute power and animal cunning.

'You've got guns, Ringo.'

'I won't use them. You have the word of a fellow-killer. C'mon, take the knife. Pretend I'm a woman.'

Tucker's attack was so swift Ringo almost lost out in those first seconds as he was knocked off his feet and took a raking kick to the ribs as he tried to regain his balance. Tucker was too eager. He kicked again. Ringo seized the foot and twisted. It was the wounded leg. Tucker gasped but did not cry out as he staggered, enabling his adversary to rise.

Tucker snatched up a heavy metal lamp and swung it like a club. Ringo knew if the man got a clean blow in he could kill him. His strength was awesome. He'd just felt it.

'You are a nothing, Ringo,' he hissed as they circled. 'This is a grandstand play — which is all you ever do. I read you clear first day. That dead whore out there mean something to you?'

Ringo attacked in a rush to connect with a crunching right.

'Where is Calla Lee, you bastard?'

No reply. Tucker lurched drunkenly, grimacing in pain. Ringo followed up with a chopping blow to the kidneys. He smashed another to a thick neck, but Tucker was moving away and the blow only struck shoulder muscle and gristle.

Tucker threw a backhand out savagely and caught Ringo by surprise, catching him to the side of the head, numbing his jaw.

Tucker grabbed at the knife, actually got his hand on it before Ringo deliberately kicked his wounded knee. Tucker retaliated with a thumping blow to the upper chest where Ringo was still bleeding. Suddenly they were locked together in a murderous exchange of kicks and blows that continued unabated until Ringo connected with a terrible pistoning knee to the groin.

He saw the fire go out of Tucker like a snuffed light. The man showed fear for the first time as he backed up against the windows, hands raised protectively.

Ringo delivered an elbow smash and the man went through the window, vanishing with a sharp yell and a splash.

He was in the creek. Moments later he had company.

'Where's the girl?' Ringo raged, seizing the sodden shirt front. 'Where?'

Tucker gasped and grappled, encircling Ringo with renewed strength, like a drowning man. The creek was tumbling them. Tucker got a headlock and dragged him under and would not let go. Ringo realized they were sinking several feet under water, and he did not have enough air in his lungs to last. He broke one arm free, slammed his elbow to the face, then kicked to the surface. Tucker bobbed up alongside and tried to kick away, might have succeeded but for the incredible pain in his right arm.

He screamed as he jerked the arm up to find only a gushing red stump where his hand had been.

Ringo's left hand seized him by the throat and dragged him into knee-deep water close to the bank. The knife was enormous in his right fist.

'Game's over,' he panted. 'You hurt me sunshine, I'll hurt you.'

The blade tore Tucker's chest open. He screamed in terror and now his face was split wide. Tucker kept his knives scalpel-sharp. Tendons, sinews and living flesh were ripped asunder in a flurry of lightning slashes, until all that was left was the killing stroke.

'You'd like it to be quick, wouldn't you?' Ringo snarled into his face. 'Karen would have liked it that way too.'

The knife plunged handle-deep into the pit of the screaming killer's belly. It ripped upwards before striking the sternum bone and bouncing out. Bobbing away in red water, Tucker couldn't even scream as his intestines floated after him.

★ ★ ★

Without strength, with barely enough will to keep himself afloat, Ringo allowed himself to be swept away by the icy torrent. There was no telling how far he floated until he felt himself slowly sliding under, then the hand on his back. Semi-conscious, he snarled and threw a weak blow that missed.

Then, 'Jesse, it's all right. It's me.'

Calla Lee's face swam above him, like an angel's.

10

TWELVE-BULLET JUSTICE

Colonel Patterson was standing taller by the day.

Having been ordered to Hudville with the regiment by his superiors in the wake of the troubles, he'd found this normally quiet and peaceful Monroe County town in turmoil. He found it hard to come to terms with doctors and morticians working overtime, important people dead and others facing serious charges. This was plainly no assignment to hand a broken-down garrison commander shuffling towards early retirement. Or was it? Seemed to everyone that once the colonel realized the full scope of what had erupted here, the violence that signified the end of the Free Lands' gun-running and rustling plagues, he seemed to get the whiff of hope for better times ahead and acted accordingly.

Arrests were made, charges presented, attorneys, prosecutors and judges summoned to make sense of the chaos and deal with those responsible. The town was cleaned up. The revitalized Patterson insisted business return to normal and had his troopers posted on the streets day and night to ensure that Hudville's recovery would be seen for what it was, namely a symbol of a return to optimism and peace throughout all Wyoming Territory.

There remained, of course, many thorny problems to be ironed out and mysteries to solve, and he eventually came to grips with a major one of these one morning five days later, as Ringo saddled his government horse at the City Livery.

The colonel and the gunfighter went a long way back. Back to the days, in fact, when a baby-faced Ringo and a saddle-tough Osage Smith had scouted for the Sixth, and done a damn fine job of it too.

Although subtly aware that an Agency operative was regarded as answerable only to his superiors, Patterson was still uneasy about much that had taken place and genuinely wanted to sit down and have a long and detailed conversation with the gunfighter in an effort to fill in the blank spaces.

He was out of luck.

Ringo was amiable, almost affable, even if to this man, who knew him well, his manner did not quite ring true. But he had nothing to say. He made a point of advising he would be returning to Agency, this despite the fact that Colonel Patterson half-suspected that he had been responsible for the deaths of at least one Agency killer during the holocaust. But he didn't have proof or witnesses, and when Jesse Ringo looked you in the eye and told you he had nothing to say, even a renewed and rejuvenated pony-soldier commander was inclined to sigh, shrug and turn his attention to easier challenges.

Ringo visited the cemetery with Calla Lee one last time, then saw her on to the stage. She wept and did not understand. He had persuaded her to put the ranch up for sale and go live with her doting uncle in San Diego, far from Wyoming and the memories. She told him she loved him one last time; he said he would never forget her and had never meant anything more in his life. She did not know he was planning to throw all chance of securing his full pardon. But what he must do, must be done.

For her, for people like her, for the Territory and the law.

★   ★   ★

The Sweetgrass Horseman's Club boasted the finest food and drink in town, was a perfect venue in which to reflect on a task well done along with today's affirmation of a generous continuance of government funding ensuring Agency's future.

Although Westerman and Carmody rarely socialized together, tonight was a special occasion, and they did so with gusto and good cheer. Hudville may have been messy and certainly proved costly. But they had it on good report that Patterson was cleaning up very effectively and their superiors had bestowed the ultimate stamp of approval on the whole affair in the only way that counted, with cash and the continuity of employment.

They were half-way through their second bottle of best French red, flushed and almost jocose as they finished off the sweets and lit the cigars in their private booth with windows overlooking sleepy streets. Carmody had begun to recount yet another 'amusing' story of events in Hudville, now viewed as a stunning victory for Agency's brutally effective way of dealing with awkward situations, when the door opened and both men looked up with their smiles freezing on their faces.

'Ringo!' Carmody was trying to

retrieve his smile but the challenge was beyond him. 'Er . . . ah, splendid to see you, Jesse. Great to see you looking so hale and hearty when we were not even certain if you had survived. Isn't it great to see Ringo back home safe and sound, Chief?'

'Wonderful,' affirmed Westerman. Yet he did not sound so .sure. Every working day of his life this silver-haired and fatherly man dealt with men who lived by the gun. He had become skilled at reading their moods, understanding them. To the casual eye an expressionless Jesse Ringo might have appeared relaxed enough, yet Chief Westerman felt himself beginning to chill from the feet up as their eyes met and held. 'Er, do take a seat, young fellow. Carmody, you might order some fresh wine. This is an occasion.'

'I don't drink with dead men.'

They were not sure they had heard aright. Had he said what they thought? Or, if so, was it some kind of joke?

'Pardon, Jesse?' Carmody's handsome features were pale and growing paler. For he had been there, unlike his superior. At the cutting edge. At Rolling Nine ranch where people had died and from where he had fled after glimpsing Tucker's corpse, gutted like a lobster, floating past his window in the east wing of the Rainsford house.

Ringo drew both Colts.

'I guess you have to do what you have to do, but not murder women. But this will help them rest easier . . . the whole Territory for that matter.'

They could not believe it.

'But . . . but what about your pardon, Ringo,' Carmody gasped, his hands slipping below the table. 'Aren't you forgetting your agreement with the governor? You did wonderfully well, you're understandably a little overwrought now, but don't throw away your passport to a normal life and a clean slate because of a little accident. And that is all Mrs Rainsford's unfortunate demise was. An accident.'

They waited for his reaction. There wasn't any. Arms folded, Ringo was a still-life figure carved out of bronze with only steel-blue eyes showing life.

In the awful silence that hung and deepened, Westerman slowly realized what was about to happen. He framed the agonized word 'No!' with bloodless lips, saw the sudden leap of intent in Carmody's face and realized he had but one hope of staying alive.

He grabbed at his shoulder holster as a snarling Carmody burst erect with a blue-barrelled .38 in his fist.

The sound of a pair of Colt .45s opening up in the confined space of a private room in a refined gentlemen's club in a small town on a quiet winter's night, came fearfully loud, like the hammers of God pounding out a clashing requiem. Four shots. None missed. The private room of the Horseman's Club was wreathed in gunsmoke as Ringo strolled out past stunned staff and dazed customers to pass unchallenged into the night.

★ ★ ★

The Rockies were behind him and winter was drawing on. Ringo turned up the collar of his sheepskin and patted the government horse between the ears. By now the wanted dodgers would be papering the trees of the territory and they would be hunting for him for the rest of his life. He'd realized this before the Sweetgrass showdown, yet knew he would do it again. To kill a snake you must get the head — Agency's own axiom. If you failed to get the head, you would be responsible for the next man the reptile killed.

Yet he sensed the violence and killing might be over; for himself, certainly, for the territory, hopefully. He would not be reforming, just changing. For a miracle had happened in Monroe County. Someone had cared for him and he'd let himself care for someone for the very first time since watching his mother and father vanish from his life to join an artist's colony in Chihuahua.

He smiled. The impossible had happened, and he always believed that what could happen once could happen again. And even if not, he would always have memories of pretty Calla Lee.

He rode on across Utah's snowy wilderness with the mighty mountains at his back. Jesse Ringo, fugitive and free man. Alone again yet easy in his mind. Riding out a long Utah afternoon to vanish slowly and for ever into the mists, the myths and the legends of the West.